THE *Sweetest* TEMPTATION

CHERYL BARTON

Books by Cheryl Barton
www.cherylbarton.net
www.crbarton.com
Upcoming Novels

Bachelor Series
(all on Kindle Unlimited)
(In Order)
Bachelor Not for Sale
A Designed Affair
A Perfect Combination
Love at Last

Brothers of Chi-Town
(In Order)
I Can't Let Go
Swagger and Baggage
Claiming His Child
Always Bet on Black
It Takes Two to Tangle
Crashing into Love
Leaks, Lies, Lust and Love
A Debt of Love

The Sullivans of Montana
(In Order)
Home for Thanksgiving
The Way You Love Me
On the Right Track
Three's a Crowd
The Law of Love

Sister Act
(In Order)
An Unexpected Destiny
For You I Will
More Than Friends

Amorous Occupations
(In Order)
The Artist
The Bookkeeper
The Chef
The Dancer
The Electrician
*The First Baseman

A Lovers' Heart
Heartthrob
Heartbeat
Heartbreaker

Stand Alone Romance

Snowbound
Cupid's Arrow
One Wish
His Halloween Promise
Holly for Christmas
A Better Man
Bossy
Un-Break My Heart
Love on Top
Take a Knee
Love at First Sight
My First Love
Black Love
A Younger Man
The Lake House
True Lies or True Love
When I Think of You
Baby, Come Back
Unforgettable
And Then There Was You
Dashing Through the Snow
One Moment in Time
The Power of Seduction
Seize the Moment
Being Neighborly
A Christmas Wish
It Should Have Been You
The Christmas Layover
The Diner
The Sweetest Revenge
The Sweetest Temptation
The Real Deal
A Prescription for Love

1

Gabrielle Mann stood on the outside of the stadium doors where, in a matter of hours, she would kick off the first night of her four concerts in Miami, Florida. She was ready for the lights, camera and action that comes along with her live performance. This is why she works so hard. What's going happen on the other side of that door is her life. Bright lights and big stages are synonymous with her name. As her father, William Mann, would often remind her, she was made for this.

Despite the fact that she'd been in many concert venues and arenas throughout her burgeoning career as a singer and possibly up and coming actress, she always entered each place with a newness in her spirit and a zeal for entertaining in her heart. She could feel it practically trying to beat outside of her chest. This type of nervousness often overcame her on the first night of a tour in a new city.

She's performed in Miami before. Still, this time felt as new as her first time. Her routine was her staple.

Tonight's concert was the next to the last city of her sold out tour that started almost a year ago, her first as a headliner. After two years as an opening act and now a number one hit release, at twenty-six, that spoke volumes.

When she was eighteen and graduating from Sierra Canyon School in Los Angeles, California, her home town, all she could think about, even back then, was her dream of one day seeing her own name large and lit up above a stage. She still couldn't believe she was a star. She loved being on stage from as far back as elementary school when she got her first taste of being celebrated because of her gift of singing. She had been asked to sing a Christmas song when she was in the second grade. Afterward, everyone in the auditorium was on their feet and cheering for her. That was the moment she and her family knew that she had talent. She'd been on a path to stardom since then.

Growing up, there were plays and recitals in school for years. Church choir, community shows and plays became a norm for her. She loved being a part of it all. Being a headlining star was just the next step on her path to happiness. For an instant, she thought about happiness and wondered if being on stage would continue to bring that to her life. When her mind drifted to what would really make her happy, images of the perfect man distracted her. Shaking that off, she turned her attention back to the doors which were still closed. This was not the moment to rehash a love that never came to fruition. It happens, she thought.

Staring at the doors in front of her, she was doing what she did in every city where she performed. She was standing on the highest-level waiting for the crew to open the door, giving her a first look at the stage from the furthest point away.

Her team, who are responsible for making sure everything is ready for every one of her shows thought her ritual of seeing the concert arena before any fans arrived was crazy. Not once has she ever discovered an issue with anything. That wasn't why she insisted on seeing everything from the highest point. It was her priority that every person who paid money to see her in concert got a magnificent view. If the place had any kind of obstructed view, she made sure that no seats were sold in those sections.

"Are you going inside?"

Gabby, the name that everyone called her, looked over her shoulder at Sierra Casey, one of her best friends who was also in the entertainment industry. Sierra, along with her childhood best friend, Victoria Knight, were her biggest and greatest supporters outside of her family. Sierra was often too busy to take in her shows, but as luck would have it, she was shooting a pilot for a new show in Miami. The moment Gabby knew that her tour would hit Miami, she told Sierra so that they could connect and maybe hang out after the show. Miami was a party city and she loved a party.

"You made it!" Gabby shouted as she was being pulled into a hug. "Did you have a problem getting in?" she asked.

"No and it shouldn't have been as easy as it was. Especially knowing that there is a crazy man out to wife you or whatever he's trying to do besides being damn scary," Sierra snorted.

"You should have Marcia get you some better security. She the record label executive who travels with you to most of your shows. The expectation is that she should be doing a better job."

"I know. I will. Tonight, I only want to have fun. You know how I get before a show. I don't want any drama. I do expect people to do the jobs they are being paid to do, especially my leadership team and my security."

Just then, the doors in front of her opened and she got her first look inside. Everything was lit up as it would be for her entrance. Her background singers were in place at their microphones. Her dancers were moving about so that she could make sure they were seen from her vantage point.

"Everything looks great from here. I love it. Do you love it?" Sierra asked.

"I do. It's amazing, isn't it? I still pinch myself sometimes. There are days when it's hard to believe I'm really at this stage of my career at twenty-six."

"You've worked hard. Your dedication to your craft and your fans has paid off. I've seen your rehearsals. Being on stage is your lane. All that energy you put into your shows is why the fans follow you from city to city. Damn the haters who want to talk about you dressing too sexy or too slutty. I've even seen comments about how you move your body and the attention it garners. You have the body a lot of women wish they could have been naturally born with like you were; so, use it. They can't come for your vocals though. That voice of yours is unmatched. People have already labeled you the new *'voice'* now that Whitney Houston's gone."

"Whew, how I miss her. I still spend hours listening to her music. I believe her *Just Whitney* CD was her best. It's definitely my favorite. Her songs, *Tell Me No* and *Unashamed* are played daily when I'm listening to music."

"I've heard you sing those songs. You've definitely got pipes just like she had."

Gabby looked back at the stage, which was lit up in purple. Even her name in lights was that color. After all, purple was her favorite color. She changed her stage colors up from one city to the next depending on the colors she chose to wear, which changed often. Her last show, over a week ago, was in Chicago. The sign and stage colors started out red. When she was in Houston, it was green.

"I love what I see. Let's head to my dressing room to relax

before the show. Besides, you know how nervous I get in the hours before I hit the stage," Gabby admitted.

"Grapes?" Sierra asked.

Her close friends knew her so well.

"You know it! I ordered red and green grapes. It's the only thing that settles my nerves before a big show. That and my pink lemonade."

As they walked, Gabby's high-heels clicked on the concrete floor. At a statuesque, five-foot-eight, with heels on, she was a little over six-feet tall. She loved the height the shoes she loved wearing the most gave her.

"I love this outfit. I swear a bodysuit was made for your body. You've got natural curves in all the right places. Most of us women, to stay looking as good as you, have to secretly get some kind of surgery. Not that there is anything wrong with that, but you, my friend, were born with beauty, brains and body – a woman made for the spotlight."

Gabby had heard that from a lot of women. Her mother taught her at an early age to love the skin the Lord blessed her to be born in. She didn't care how it turned out as she got older, it was all about taking care of the temple. Her mother, at sixty-two was still naturally beautiful. She only hoped she could be that sexy at that age one day, even after having three children.

"Thanks, girl. You know I appreciate you. You're what, thirty-two? You're already getting surgery done? You look amazing just as you are. You're on a hot new show in its second season. There is already talk of two more seasons coming even though you all just started recording season two. That's major. People love all of you just as you are. If you change anything, do it for you and not for anyone else, especially social media critics who spend their days worrying about how you live your life."

Entering her dressing room, Gabby plopped down on the large purple chaise lounge that had been brought in especially for her. Sierra headed straight for the table full of veggies, cheeses and fruits. Gabby never liked heavy food before a show.

"Is Victoria coming to this show?" Sierra asked, making a plate for her and one for Gabby before sitting across from her on a long pink and white sofa.

"No, but she's planning to come to my final show in Los Angeles."

"I can't wait to see her again. We have such a good time when the three of us are together. I'm sorry I'll miss the last leg of your tour. That's happening during my full week of taping. I'll be catching it all on social media. I'm sure everyone will have a camera out. I miss the days of people focusing more on the entertainment in front of them than on recording it to be the first to post it. Those were the good ol' days!" Sierra joked. "Did I tell you that Terri wants me to think about taking singing lessons? She said I could expand my reach when it comes to role offers if I extended my talent beyond acting. What has she said to you about acting?"

Gabby nodded. She and Sierra had the same agent, which is how they met. They had both been booked for the same time slot for a meeting with Terri Blanchard, one of the top agents to the stars. It had been an error, but they had instantly become best friends while waiting for Terri's last meeting to end, which was always the case.

"She's lining up some readings for me. I'm still thinking it over. I would love to get into some acting, but then I look at all of my free time I'd be giving up chasing after that. I would love to have a year of doing absolutely nothing."

"Are you burning out already?"

"No. This tour has been a lot, though. I'm loving it, but I can't wait for it to end. I don't want to have to rise in the morning to an alarm because I have get dressed and run from one meeting or appointment to the next. My brother and my father are heading into new political territory. I want to be able to support them too. My dad is going to become the Senate majority leader. My brother is looking forward to running for Governor. He is the youngest to ever sit in that seat, but he is in it because as Lt. Governor, when Governor Hastings died in that plane crash five months ago, my brother assumed his position. For the upcoming election, he'll have to run. He's pretty much won already. He's running unopposed. People remember the great things my dad did as Governor of California and they believe my brother is a chip off that old block."

"Besides being fine as hell! Jordan Mann is a gift to all women's eyes. Too bad he has a steady girlfriend. He's not married though, so maybe there is hope for me and your brother to fall in love yet," Sierra joked.

"My brother's girlfriend is the best. He's the lucky one. He snagged himself one of the top models in the world. He's not letting her go. If they both slow down long enough, my mother is hoping for the second wedding in our family. My oldest brother Chadwick is living a blissful life with his wife, Sade and my nephews, Denton and Micah. Life is good in the Mann family."

"Is it? Does that mean for you too?"

Gabby gave Sierra the eye. It was her sign that told Sierra

to not try to read her on her personal life.

"You know my story. Not yet, but look at me – I'm irresistible," she quipped, laughing off the comment.

"Yeah, you are! You just have to stop being so picky."

"You call Adonis Duquette being picky? You know better."

"Oh, snap. You said his whole name. I haven't heard you say it in a while."

"I try not to. Remember, I'm Leo's girl, even if it's not real. I still have to keep up the image."

"I hear you. Have you seen or heard from Adonis, lately?"

"No. I did see him in the crowd when Jordan was sworn in. I looked back a second time and he was gone; just like that. That man can get in and out of a place and you'd be fooled into questioning if he was ever really there."

"Maybe there is still hope for the two of you. Is DJ K-Line still opening for you tonight? She is one bad ass DJ!"

"That she is. She should be setting up shortly. They'll move my set back so that she can get hers set up. I think she's running a bit behind. She had a show last night in Jacksonville and got a late start this morning. I trust that she'll be on time. She knows how I like to start exactly when my fans expect us to. They trust me with their time. If K-Line is late, her set will be shorter; she knows that. That's why she makes sure she's on time."

Sierra nodded her head enthusiastically.

Gabby knew that her friend could relate to people being on-time and how important that was. Some headliners don't mind starting late, even if the delay wasn't their fault. She didn't have any of that. The people she worked with actually appreciated her promptness.

"I meant to ask you about Victoria's decision to move to

the west coast. I know she is your assistant and usually flies all over with you. She still makes her homebase in New York?"

"She's ready to get up out of there. She's the best and I don't trust anyone in that position but someone who knows all of me. That is the good, bad, ugly and indifferent things about me; all that quirky stuff. My label loves the work she does for me directly and are interested in having her come onboard full-time for them. The money would be stupid crazy to pass up. She's thinking about it."

"Bring me up to date on you and Leo – the biggest 'It' couple in the industry right now. Have the two of you sealed any kind of deal yet? I know you're not a real couple or even in a relationship, but from what I've heard about him, that brother knows how to scratch any itch a woman has."

"Absolutely not. It's not that kind of party. We are two sexy people who are connected romantically for the sake of our careers. It works out great for us both. It's definitely boosted both of our images. Our linkage also brings out the crazies who either want me away from him so that they could have him, or they want him away from me thinking that he is their block from getting to me. *Not!*"

The mood in the room changed quickly. Gabby had shared with Sierra about the stalker who is getting more brazen with his attempts to get under her skin. She's never experienced anyone so fixated on her before. She didn't like it but knew it came with the territory.

"It's still going on, huh?" Sierra asked, talking about the horrible letters, emails and other things she's been getting.

"Well, at first, the letters were love letters. He was talking about how much he loves me and wants to be with me. Then when Leo and I got together, his contact started to turn more dangerous, violent even, but only toward me."

"That's because Leo's guys would pulverize this guy if he came after him. Men tend to think of women as easier targets to terrorize into submission."

"Yeah, I know. The wildest thing is this guy seems to know a lot about my comings and goings and not just what is put up on social media or on my website. He knows childhood things that make him seem even creepier. Nothing is as menacing though, as what I've been getting for the past few months. He attempted to have black flowers covered in blood delivered to me. Turns out it's the blood of a cat or something like that. It means he would have had to get blood from a cat somehow. Just crazy. The letters are changing in their tone, as well," she explained.

"Girl, who the hell is still out here writing letters?" Sierra joked in her attempt to lighten up the mood.

Gabby appreciated that considering how much of a damper the entire issue could bring to her view of it all. She was doing her best to cope.

"Not really hand written. They are typed letters, but still, who does that still either?" Gabby jested.

Their conversation was about to continue when the sound of Leo calling her name through the door stirred their attention toward him. He entered and Gabby watched his eyes right on her. She also saw that usual gleam that meant he had more on his mind with her than just saying hello before they hit the stage together.

"Hey beautiful!" he said, entering with three of his line-backer looking bodyguards with him.

"Hey yourself," Gabby replied.

"Hey, Sierra."

"Hey, Leo. You're fly as usual. Do people still say that?" Sierra quipped.

"They do and I appreciate the sentiment. I try to do what I can do every time I can do it. Both of you look lovely. Gabby, I can't see the full impact of that white bodysuit on you, but damn, from what I can see, you look as gorgeous as always. You ready for tonight's show?" he asked, taking a seat next to her on the chaise lounge, which was actually only made for one person.

She hated how aggressive he was with her private space. It was all a part of never stepping away from the disguise of the fake relationship. Leo never let it go. She only went on full-force in front of the public. He held onto it even in private settings as well. She knew exactly why.

Though she carried on with the façade, Leo has made it clear on more than one occasion that he would like a relationship with her to be real. She wasn't having it. She knew that, secretly, he was already in four to five relationships; none of them serious. She wouldn't be a play thing for him; something he's known for. He wasn't fooling her. She would not be another high-profile woman that he could put a check next to on his list. She was happily on no one's list.

"I'm always ready," she said.

"I see you have your organic grapes. I guess you are. Listen, can we talk shop for a few? I'm going to hit the stage for my microphone check. Before I did that, I wanted to chat. Is that okay?"

When he looked in Sierra's direction, Gabby knew what that meant. Leo didn't want to talk shop. He wanted a chance to make another play for her. She would give him his five minutes. She learned early on that it's best to let Leo say his peace in order to get it out of his system.

"I'm going to let the two of you talk. I need to make a few phone calls. I'll see you from the side of the stage, Gabby. I know you'll knock their socks off as usual. Leo, keep it tight," she said before leaving the room.

Gabby wanted to laugh out loud but didn't. Sierra had said words that were a joke just between them. She used to tell Leo to keep it hanging, but they both know that he was more comfortable when he kept it slanging.

Leo was fine. Women threw themselves at him relentlessly. When he found one who could keep a secret, he put his guys on her. That was his way of operating.

His team left out behind Sierra leaving them alone.

When he leaned over in her direction, Gabby stood and walked over to the table to grab a bottle of water. She stayed there and turned toward him.

"Still?" he asked.

"Leo, stop it. You had to know I was going to move. When have I not moved when you've tried to make a move on me. Does that really work on women? I guess when they gaze into your dreamy eyes and you sing sweet-like to them, they fall for everything."

Leo laughed and crossed his legs, placing a hand on his knee and the other under his chin.

"Ah, but you're immune to me, right? I don't get it. We're in a perfect position to make something happen. The world already thinks something is going on. Why not dip our feet into the deep end and give it a try?" he asked.

"Boy, every part of you is already in deep ends all over the world. Stop playing thinking I'm that girl. I'm not a groupie. You have enough of those."

"Sexy, I'm just saying that it could get lonely on the road. We could be each other's stand-in."

"Leo, what we have is for show. Don't forget that."

"It doesn't have to be."

"Yes, it does."

"Are you seeing someone?"

"I'm not going there with you. You know how private I am," she retorted.

"True, but if there is a slip-up, it could ruin what we are building career-wise. Our fans will never come back if they find out we've been lying to them. They love seeing us together. You having a whole other man out here could hurt us. I have a proposition for you," he offered.

"Another one? Also, why would a man be a crutch for me that could ruin us, but the long list of hotel squeezes I know you entertain are not?" she asked.

Leo did laugh out loud that time.

"Busted. Look, you said that and I immediately heard it as if DJ Khalid had said it. That's one of his famous lines."

"Yeah, well, you clearly have some lines too."

"Woman, you are wearing the hell out of that bodysuit. Tell the brother who is getting all of that, that he is the world's luckiest man. I see why your confidence is through the roof. You know you're fine. I'm saying, give me a shot."

Gabby shook her head no. She wasn't falling for it.

She didn't get a chance to answer further before there was a knock on the door.

"Leo, your rehearsal time is here. Let's go, man," Darius, his head of security yelled through the door.

Leo stood to leave. When he attempted to walk toward her, she put up her hand to stop him.

"For public display only," she warned him.

Leo raised his hands in surrender and backed up toward the door.

"I got you. I mean no harm. I really do come in peace."

"Before you expound on that, don't. I see the wheels turning in your head on how you can turn those words into something vulgar. Remember who you're talking to," she said reminding him of the lines he agreed to not cross when he signed his contract like she did about their fake love affair.

"Fair enough. I'll see you out on the stage. I'm telling you that you have no idea what you're missing out on."

"Oh, I am quite sure that I do. I've heard the stories. I'm good, trust me."

When he opened the door, Darius entered with a huge bouquet of purple flowers. She assumed they were from Leo and she thanked him. He must not have heard her because he was already out of the door without responding.

Setting the flowers down for a minute to check her phone, she thought about her mention of Adonis earlier during her talk with Sierra. She wished things had turned out differently. She secretly wished that the man she'd given her heart to, though he didn't know it, back when she was a teenager would come for her the way Leo keeps trying to do. Adonis is the man she wants. The fact that he didn't feel the same way about her was still disheartening eight years later. That time in her life hit her like a ton of bricks. She never wanted to relive that time when her heart got broken. Adonis had succeeded in shattering it into a million pieces when he rejected her. He may be her brother's best friend, but that should not have stopped them from being involved. Adonis never gave her a reason other than telling her no and suggesting that her crush would go away one day. To her dismay, it never has. She hated that she still loved him as much now as she did at eighteen. At fifteen, it was a teenage crush. By eighteen, she only had eyes for him.

Remembering the flowers from Leo, she picked them up and sniffed them. Oddly, they didn't have a smell at all, though they were beautiful. She removed the card from the envelope and read it. Her skin felt like knives were sticking into her as she read:

"Have a good show my love. If Leo touches you again in any way on that stage, I'm going to kill you for letting it happen. There could be a casket with your name on it. I love you."

Gabby dropped the flowers to the floor and screamed. In an instant, her head of security, Sonny, burst through the door. She pointed to the flowers and the note that were on the floor. He read it.

"I'm sorry Gabby. I saw Leo's guy with them and thought they were from Leo."

She couldn't respond. Instead, she grabbed her phone, with tears in her eyes and called her brother. Whoever had sent the flowers was getting too close.

"Get them out of here!" she yelled.

He rushed around picking them up.

"Sure thing. Again, I'm sorry. I'll find out how his security got them and why they would deliver them here without running a strange delivery by your team. I'm on it," he yelled before running out of the room.

"No one in and no one out other than Ms. Sierra. You got it?" Sonny said, questioning his team before the door shut.

The moment Jordan answered the phone, Gabby burst

into tears. For the first time in a long time, she felt vulnerable. She felt all alone. She was frightened like never before.

2

Adonis Duquette leaned back in the conference room chair at the table that sat sixteen, but only two remained. A man he trained with years ago and ran several operations with as members of a special team of CIA agents, Jaycion Jackson, special forces code name, Cypher, sat across from him. They decided to remain after several team members debriefed on each of their cases. Adonis sighed deeply as he tried to digest the fact that he was being forced to take at least six-months of downtime. He was instructed to do so in order to regroup for his next assignment. His last one had him undercover for over a year, his longest stint so far.

Agents his age at thirty-one, aren't usually as deep under as he was. With the code name, Jaguar, given to him the minute he was recruited into the agency during his first year of college, another rare circumstance, he was known for having a keen sense for hunting his prey. He was able to sidle up to someone without detection until he was already on them.

Like him, Cypher was assigned extraordinary cases with dangerous and extenuating circumstances. That meant a lot of time away from family and friends. In the end, taking a respite was no longer an option, it was a requirement.

"Forced relaxation is the worst!" Adonis yelped after pounding his fist on the table out of frustration.

"What? You mean you want to fight against going home to spend time either with family or alone to reorganize your mind for duty? These assignments are hard. You know they're on us about our mental health," Jaycion explained.

"Yeah, I got that speech during my required post-assignment therapy session. I was cleared with no long-lasting effects of a long undercover assignment. That should tell them I'm fine. I'm not pushing back, though. I could use some time at my place in Los Angeles. It's been a while since I've been home for any long period of time. The last was for a few hours when Jordan was sworn in as Governor of California."

"A few hours? Oh, yeah, I remember. You were defiant in the instruction to not go."

"I had to go. You know that Jordan is like a blood brother to me. He and his family are the only family I have. When his father was Governor, he snatched me out of a life that was heading in the wrong direction. I wouldn't have missed Jordan's big day."

"I understand that. You and I are similar in our upbringing. The streets of Baltimore were nothing to play about. It was kill or be killed. I can remember having a gun in my hand at ten-years-old," Jaycion explained.

"Where are you headed after this?"

Adonis would like nothing more than to head out for his next assignment, but he got what his director was saying. For the past four years, he'd gone from one case to another. That took him to various parts of the world to handle the business of his country. In his heart, he knew he needed a break. Cypher wasn't being forced to take time, but he was asking for some space to handle something personal.

"Something big is going down in my hometown with some people I care about very much. I'm hoping to insert myself in it to keep them alive. After that, my plan is to take a little downtime myself. I may take you up on your office to see the ocean on that coast when my eyes aren't only focused on work. How are the businesses coming along?"

Adonis nodded and smiled. The best decision he'd ever made was to invest his money in a friend's lucrative automobile customization business. Trent Basheer, like Jordan, was a brother-figure in his life. Trent's father, Houston Basheer, had been a business partner of Jordan's father in a chain of exclusive country clubs. Houston, in his will, had left him a substantial amount of money to do with as he pleased just like he had done with his own children. Adonis and Houston talked often before he died. The father-figure told him how proud he was of his desire to serve his country. He wanted to help him get set up for life if and when he decided to retire from a field that could have him sacrificing his life. Adonis had invested the money well. One of those investments was with Trent and a few business ventures he'd gotten off the ground years ago. One such business which started out as one auto shop five years ago was now seven shops across the Los Angeles area.

"Growing by leaps and bounds. Trent and the guys have taken the shops to new heights. I don't get to be a part of the day-to-day, but my part in the business is making sure I continue to bring in new customers. Like you!" he joked.

"The upgrades they made to my charger were beyond

anything I could have imagined. I'm still thinking about a bike like yours. I've been meaning to ask, with a code name like Jaguar, do you actually own a Jaguar?" Jaycion asked.

I own a 2020 Porsche 911 Carrera in black that Trent is finishing up some customizations on. I'm hoping to put that on the highway when I get home to test how many speeding tickets I can get. You know that we don't get to enjoy our toys like the average American citizen does because of how little time we get outside of work."

"Including women, right?"

Adonis shook his head from side to side. He's had his share of women, but because of his career, he hasn't settled down with any one woman. Instead, he prefers to enjoy the company of women who know he has no plans for commitment. That is, unless he would one day come to his true reality about one woman in particular.

"That's the biggest downfall along with being a high about this job. Lately, I've been wondering about the things I'm missing out on in life like coming home to that one woman; even children. I mean, do I even want any?" Adonis questioned.

"I hear you on that. Like me, of course you do. That's another long conversation. I have a woman who I haven't been able to get out of my head since I was about fourteen or fifteen years old. She's a hard one to let go of. She's also the only woman that makes it hard for me to keep her close. I've had the same thoughts that you've had. I believe we're entitled to have that good woman who will love us and the career that we've chosen. It's a part of the struggle and the fight that we need to be willing to have. The question is, how bad do we want lives outside of chasing danger and the rush of adrenalin we get out of that? We have jobs we love, we have money, we have things, but it looks like the idea of the family foundation – a woman and children, appear to be out of our reach. That's not because it has to be that way, but perhaps, we're not fighting as hard for it as we do against forces that threaten this country. You mentioned your lady a few times to me; the one who doesn't know your true feelings about her. I'm hoping you'll think long and hard about it while you're enjoying your respite. She's based out of Los Angeles when she's not touring, right?"

Adonis didn't share that all he's been doing lately is thinking about her; day and night. Even more now that he'll be home for a spell. As he gets older, he questions if he could have made a different choice years ago, he may be as happy in his personal life as he was in his work life. Only time would tell.

"True. Right now, she's in Miami. I keep up with her tour, but I haven't seen her in quite some time."

"She's beautiful. I've seen snippets of her concerts. She's definitely a songbird with some strong pipes. I haven't heard a woman reach those octaves since Mariah Carey or even Minnie Ripperton. Her voice is pure," Jaycion noted.

"And a heart that's pure gold. She's beauty, brains and power."

"Is it too late?"

"I think so. I'm not one of her favorite people. In fact, I would label it as hate."

They stood to leave.

"Maybe not. I'll tell you what; if you don't give up on your lady, I won't give up on mine. Deal?"

Adonis shook the hand that his friend and partner in crime

placed before him.

"Deal. I'm going to hold you to paying me a visit. We'll grill some steaks and toss back more beers than we're allowed to drink while working."

As he reached the doorway, Adonis' phone rang. The moment he saw that it was Jordan, he stepped back into the room and told Jaycion that he'd catch up with him later.

"Jordan, brother – how the hell are you? I guess you remembered my text to you letting you know I'd be back in the states for a few months, specifically in L.A."

"I did remember. The timing is impeccable. Whether that's good or bad still remains to be seen with why I'm calling you. I know you were looking to just relax, but I need your help with something. I can't ask anyone but you. I feel bad that I'm asking you to use your profession for my personal need. I've never done that before."

"There is absolutely nothing I wouldn't do for you and you know that. If it's related to my profession, I won't feel so useless trying to figure out how to relax for at least the next six months," he quipped.

"That's how long you'll home? How are you feeling? Your mind straight?" Jordan asked.

"That's to start with. This last assignment was tough. I've had my evaluations and they're all good. Even though I was signed off and can continue my duties, I was told, not asked, to lay low for a few months and do something fun."

"Fun? What's that?" Jordan joshed.

They laughed together.

"Exactly. What do you have for me that you're stalling with? Lay it on me," Adonis said sitting back at the table.

"It's Gabby."

Adonis felt the hair on his arms stand on end. This was about Gabby?

"What's wrong? Did something happen to her?" he asked harshly.

He knew his voice sounded scratchy but he didn't care. Jordan was right. Never has he or anyone in their family ever asked him for help; especially her. For Gabby, he would do anything.

"Whoa, don't blow a gasket – I get it, trust me. It's Gabby. She's okay. No one has hurt her, at least not yet."

"What the hell does that mean? Not yet? Jordan you are slow-talking me and I hate that," he said gruffly.

Adonis was trying to control his eagerness to get them to the gist of the conversation, but it was becoming a losing battle.

"Okay. Gabby is a star so unwanted attention comes with her line of work. Even as a politician, it comes with mine. My brother, mayor of Chicago, my dad, a U.S. Senator, again, threats follow this family each and every day. With Gabby though, being the only girl and out in this world traveling and not being as focused on her surroundings as she should be, I'm always worried about her."

"What happened?"

"Last night, before the first of four shows in Miami, she called me crying. I mean she was really crying. I almost hopped on a plane, putting aside my crazy meeting schedule, just to check in on her. I think I still will, but only for tonight's show. She gets lots of messages from fans, but what's been happening lately is beyond that. Someone is threatening her. There is some guy out here who thinks Gabby belongs to him. He's beyond obsessed with her. At first there were devotions of love. I've seen some emails and letters that have all been untraceable. Local police in various jurisdictions have been made aware of what's been happening. The FBI has been notified, especially around some of the gifts that have been addressed to her that could be considered a threat. Yesterday, somehow this guy was able to have flowers and a card delivered directly to her by Leo's security detail."

Adonis fumed. He already had a few choice words for Leo, Gabby's other half.

"How the hell did that happen? His team gave her something that, what, a stranger just handed to them and said to give it to her? Where is Gabby's security? I know she doesn't have the kind that you, as a politician would have but they should be protecting her with their lives. Nothing should slip through."

"I hear you. That's what I'm saying too. There are things I haven't told you. I know she hasn't told you because, well, we know what that's about. I can't believe she's still mad at you. It's been like eight years or so. Anyway, when she was in Chicago, she received a celebratory cake from the hotel staff. They told her it was sent by me to congratulate her on a successful tour. The cake actually made it to her room. She said the moment she saw it, she knew it wasn't from me. I would never send her a cake with chocolate icing. Though she loves chocolate, she hates it on a cake. When she called me, I told her it wasn't from me. Under the cake was a note that said something like 'a sweet for my sweetie. Eat it all, but save some icing for...' I won't go into what was next. It was quite vulgar. There have been a lot of this and from the same person. How he's able to bypass her security I don't know. How he's able to know exactly where she's staying or the road she's on, I'm clueless. When I speak of the road, he was able to have a billboard put up on the route her travel bus was taking. No one should have known about that. Somehow, he's a step ahead at all times. I'm worried."

"As you should be."

"Gabby, on the other hand, at first brushed it off. You know her – she's the party queen. She goes out, sometimes even giving her security detail the slip. She's young, I get it, but she's being careless too. Her security could be better. I've been saying that to her record label for a while now. If I could legally provide her with the kind of security that I have, I would. My family and I are trying to let her be independent enough to make her own decisions so that she trusts those in her camp. Between me and you, they just let her do whatever she wants because she's a big star. The label wants to keep her happy so that she keeps pumping out number one hits."

"That's not worth the risk to her," Adonis inserted.

"Exactly. She went on a bike ride one day with her security team following her in their truck. She was sick of them being around and darted through a park. They lost her. She thought it was funny; they did not. And neither did I. I don't know. I'm trying to be patient, but I'm getting scared. I heard the fear in her voice last night. I remembered you were coming home. I don't want to intrude on your time. I need your help."

"What do you need?"

Gabby is one person that Jordan should assume he wouldn't say no to or about. She was his person; even if he's never confessed that to her.

"I would love to say if you can talk to her about the outfits she wears at her shows, that would be a start. They are so revealing that as her brother, I'm giving her the side eye when

25

I see her on stage. There's just so much skin. She's my little sister. You know how I am about her."

Adonis has had the same kind of thoughts but from a different perspective. He's in love with Gabby and doesn't want any man seeing all of her body. He also understands that it's part of the role she plays. She's sitting at the top of every music chart. She's come a long way since doing local shows around Los Angeles back when she was in high school. At that time, their mother accompanied her everywhere. With their father spending most of his time in D.C., that's where their mother remained, by his side. They trust Gabby to be responsible for her own life. They also depended on her record label and management team to do right by her. Clearly, someone was missing a beat. He would also never tell Jordan that to him, Gabby looked damn-fine in those sexy outfits, but that's just him. He loved a woman who was confident to own everything about herself and did whatever she wanted. That kind of woman was a force; one he very much found himself drawn to. There is no way a woman as fine as her would not attract every man, and most women – some who would even take their obsession to a dangerous level. He took out his other cell phone and after silencing the sound, pulled up her IG page, checking out some of her latest videos. The woman shone like no other woman did on stage. She sang from some place deep down in her soul that completely mesmerized anyone who set eyes on her. Not only was her stage set up electric but so was her presence and her beauty.

"You and I both know that I'm the last person she would listen to," Adonis clarified. If anyone knew his history with Gabby, it was Jordan. He had been front and center for what happened the night of her prom.

"I know you haven't been around but let me take you back to last year's Met Gala to give you some perspective. After she and Leo made their appearance, she went out with a bunch of friends, some I don't care for at all. Thankfully Victoria was there with her."

Adonis knew all about Victoria. She and Gabby had been friends since middle school. She now worked as Gabby's main executive assistant as she traveled around the world performing.

"I think I saw something about that," he said, following the conversation.

"I should have known you would be aware of what's happening in her life. You know I wish there was more to it for you and her, but I digress. I'll leave that for you to figure out. That night, after the Gala, she was out partying without a care in the world. The next day, she received images of her that had to have been taken right next to her. This creep was a step away from her. He then sent her a message that said she needed to watch the company she keeps, especially her security because he was able to get close enough to her that his hand was seen in the pictures and video almost touching her shoulder. He wanted her to know that if he wanted to, he could have enough access to her that he could make her his at any time. He said if she didn't get her act together and stop acting like a slut that he would have to do something about it himself. That put her off, but didn't scare her to tame her wild behavior unbecoming of his woman. He said that to her. This clown has me ready to risk my job to go after him," Jordan admitted.

"This all sounds pretty scary. What was so different about last night and what she received?"

Adonis was frightened for her. Before Jordan could even get to telling him what he needed, he was already on his other phone reaching out to his travel agent by text to book him a flight to Miami immediately. He would be heading to the airport the moment he left the CIA office.

"That I don't know. It was the same sort of stuff, but it shook her up really bad. I talked to her for over an hour before I could get her to calm down before her show. I told her I was coming to town for tonight's show. I can't do anything, but I'm hoping you can."

"I'm on it."

"Okay, here is what I need. I need you to use those cat-like abilities you have of a stealth nature and check out everyone and everything about the venue. Most of all, scan for someone who stands out more than others. Her final shows are here in Los Angeles in a few weeks, but I think she's planning to make a stop at the end of this tour to her place in New York. I wish she wouldn't, but she said she wanted to hit up some party or another; I don't know. Can you get in and check out her condo there? It's a new purchase, but she doesn't spend a lot of time there. Make sure the place is as tight as Fort Knox. Remember that joke as kids?"

"I do. Like I said, I'm on it. What about her place in L.A.? Her team doesn't check any of this out?"

Adonis was disturbed. As big of a star as Gabby was, more care should be given to making sure she stays alive for another show.

"I don't know. When I try to check up on Gabby behind her back, she lays into me about trying to control her life. This is my independent sister. She's pretty bossy. She thinks that I don't trust her decision-making. Most times, I don't. If I have to see another picture of her with a drink in her hand and stumbling out of some club, I'm going to figure out how to shut it all down. Can you check out her place in L.A., too?"

"I can do that. While I'm in Miami, I'll get some guys on her place in L.A. I'll fly from Miami to New York and have a look around. I'll make sure it's all locked down tight; don't worry."

"With you at the helm, I'm not worrying about anything. Will I get a chance to see you while I'm in Miami? It will be a quick turnaround for me."

"I doubt it. You know how I move. You won't know that I'm there. Let's keep it that way. Also, don't tell Gabby I'm coming."

"I won't say anything. I will say, since you're going to be in L.A. and she'll be there too, I want her to know that I've asked you to look into the letters and other things that she's getting. You're the best at what you do. Before you tell me, I know she won't like it. I don't care. This is coming from me and my dad. He's already told me that either she goes along with it or he'll step in and cancel it all. You know my dad doesn't care if she's a grown woman or not."

"I got that. So, you want me to not just check things out on the surface, but behind the scenes, see if I can figure out who this threat is?"

"Yes. You do that every day. On this scale, this should be child's play for you. Will you do it?"

"Bro, I've just had my travel agent book my flight. I'll be in Miami ahead of tonight's show. I'll touch base with you when I'm in L.A. Does that work?"

"A.D., you're the best. You're also the best friend I could ever ask for. Gabby is lucky to have you in her corner even if she doesn't know or want you to be."

29

"We both understand why though, right?"

"A.D., be honest with me – is it really still about that at this point? I think not. I think as much as you wanted to write off Gabby's childhood crush and expressions of love to you as just that, a childhood thing, you are still denying what's really going on. Are you honestly going to tell me that the minute I said her name, terror didn't race through you? I bet your hand was on the gun at your hip."

Adonis only took his hand off of his gun when he needed to reach for his other cell phone. Jordan was right.

"I would kill anyone who even touched her without her permission."

"See? Are you going to try and convince me that though you had your own reasons back then, as the years have gone by, that you haven't fallen hard for her? I know you. I also know her. She's always talking about hating you but every time I talk to her, she asks me if I've heard from you and if you're alright. She worries about you because her love for you isn't childish. She's a woman, not a child anymore. She loves you. And you?"

Adonis felt his pulse quicken. He has fought years and years of trying to avoid conversations about his feelings for Gabby when he talks to Jordan. He didn't want to shake up their friendship. He also had a truth that he needed to get out before it ate him alive.

He pulled the phone away from his ear. He was mad that he left his earbuds in his duffle bag – his lifeline when he travels. He gasped loudly and on the other end of the phone, he heard Jordan chuckle. His friend knew.

"Jordan, you already know. Back then, I didn't want to cause any friction due to her being eighteen and me being twenty-three. My friendship with you and my love for your family is everything to me; it always has been. I wasn't good enough for your sister."

"You were and you still are. No one else is. Admit it. This is me. You being involved with my sister is the only thing I'll ever accept in this world when it comes to her and a man. I'm putting this out here so that you can hear me say it. You only have to admit that I'm right. You need to know that I'm okay with it."

"I hear you. Like I said, you already know. I'm in love with her. I have been for a few years. I may not have had much contact with her, but I have been keeping up with her. I don't know when it happened, but it did."

"You're right. I already knew. Today, is the happiest day of my life. I'll leave it to you and Gabby to work this out. In the end, I can't wait to try on my tuxedo for the wedding. See you, or not see you, in Miami."

Adonis didn't know how to respond to that when the line clicked. Jordan had hung up leaving an image in his head that he'd thought about a countless number of times. That was the first time that he'd ever said the words out loud to anyone other than himself. He was in love with Gabrielle Mann. For now, even that had to take a back seat. His priority was finding who her stalker was in order to stop him before he upped his game by following through on the promises he's made.

Jumping up, he raced out of the office to grab his duffle bag out of his locker. He had a plane to catch. He had his woman to look after.

3

Gabby was pumped for tonight's show, her second in Miami. Last night, she performed before a sold-out crowd. Again tonight, there wasn't an empty seat in the place. Reviews and social media posts about the show the previous night took over every news show and blog site. Everyone was as pumped as she was. She still couldn't believe that this was her life. Thousands of people shouted her name. Even now, as they were praying before the start of the show, she could hear the crowd screaming for her.

At the end of the prayer, everyone clapped while she took one last look at herself in the mirror. It was just below the stage where she stood waiting for her cue to start. In about five minutes, she would step on the metal platform that would slowly raise her up and above the stage to begin her performance. She looked at herself and loved what she saw. The color for the opening number tonight was all white. She had on white and silver, diamond-crusted six-inch, thigh-high boots. They made her long legs look even longer and definitely sexy. She was wearing see-through stockings that covered a thong-like, one-piece white, silver and diamond accented body suit. On her hands were rings that covered each of her fingers, connected by long chains that led to elbow cuffs with connected it to the jewelry on her fingers. She wore a diamond choker around her neck. Her ears, with five pierced holes in each, were draped in diamond cuffs that covered the entire ear. On her head was her favorite piece of her ensemble. She wore a custom-made Fedora hat in white, fully covered in diamonds. Having the hat in twelve different colors enabled her to match one with whatever color was the choice for the night. Her favorite, after the white was the hot pink and of course, the purple one. Her long hair was in very long braids that hung down her back, her favorite protective hair style. She was ready to give her audience everything in her. By way of her earpiece, she could hear her dancers giving her the encouragement that fed her actions the whole time she would be on the stage. Everyone was ready!

The show wasn't all that had her excited. Jordan, was in town and should be arriving around the same time that her show would start. Victoria had already sent her a text that Jordan was only miles away. His transportation was caught in traffic. The vetting process for his appearance at an event like this took a little extra time. He would be whisked in and straight to the side of the stage where he would have a perfect view of her show. She'd also been made aware that a safety check was being done, but she didn't know who was doing it. It wasn't like that wasn't part of the nightly routine, but she was told that this one was more detailed. After what happened the night before with the flowers, a meeting was held earlier in the day about how her security detail appeared to often be asleep on the job. With promises to do better, Gabby knew that once she told her brother what happened, something she never did because she didn't want him and her family to worry, that he would make sure there were no issues tonight. Besides, he was coming. As Governor of California, every stone was being turned over to make sure his life wasn't in jeopardy. She looked forward to bringing him out on stage to dance with her for a few minutes during her show. She didn't get to do that often because like their brother, Chad and her father, they were all busy doing their part as public servants in making life better for those who trusted them with the decisions around their welfare. She assumed the mystery security check was being done by the men and women who watched out for him every place he went.

"One minute, Gabby!" the stage manager yelled as he ran by barking out orders to everyone. She waited for him to come back to stand by her side. It was his job to make sure there were no issues with the rising of the platform. His men had already checked to be sure she was securely locked into the thin wire of the platform that would hold her in place. Rihanna, she knew, wasn't the only celebrity who could fly into the air on a platform while singing and dancing. She'd mastered that herself and her fans loved it.

"Ready?" he came back and asked.

"Let's get it!" she replied while adding her usual thumbs-up. The music blared and the crowd went wild the minute she started singing a slow ballad, a fan top favorite, as she rose in the air.

"My first love, our time has come
On a beach, on the sand, together under the sun
I call your name, my words in the air
You call me baby, I look, you stare..."

Giving them everything she knew they wanted as the song continued, Gabby let everything that tried to steal her joy the night before with the flowers and card that she couldn't seem to forget, fade away. This was her stage. This was her family. This was her time.

Behind her she felt the heat of the lights behind her that lit up massively in white. The crowd clamored for her with the lighters from their phones in the air. The words of her favorite song flowed out of her naturally. This song, *A Lover's Dare*, was a number one hit. She could hear everyone singing as loud as she was, knowing every word. There was no doubt that her fans assumed the song was about Leo. She knew better. What she and Leo shared didn't even involve kissing, let alone anything else that could lead to her writing a love song about him. No, this song was about someone else who was special to her.

As the platform moved her high, then low before going high again, she thought about the man behind the song she wrote in one sitting. The words flowed easily when an image of her and her dream man, Adonis, appeared before her eyes. Staying close to the mark on the raised platform, she sang as if he were in the venue watching her perform. As much as she wished she could move on beyond him, she has never been able to. She never questioned how this song rose on the charts so fast. Every word she sang was real. They weren't the words of a young girl, but those of a woman whose heart still belonged to one man. She wondered if he had heard the song in his treks around the world. She thought about whether he would think she was talking about him.

As the song ended and she prepared to toss her hat off of her head and to one of the stage hands below, the platform slowly lowered her down until she could step off of it. Once on solid ground, her dancers worked quick to remove the wire that held her safely in place. Her next song was a fast one. She grabbed a new microphone being handed to her as she made her way quickly to the front of the stage. She turned, bent over, looked at the crowd between her legs and as usual, they went wild. She dropped her hips all the way to the floor, swirling them as she rose with sharp, pointed moves. Flanked on both sides and behind her by sixteen dancers, she owned her stage. For the next hour, her world was the scene of thousands of people depending on her to be their outlet for the night. When she turned to the side, waving feverishly from the wings and dancing along with everyone else with him, except for his security detail, was Jordan. He made it! Her head screamed with excitement. She hadn't seen him in a month after he dropped in for about an hour during a show she had in Atlanta. That night, both of her brothers surprised her by coming to see her perform. She waved back to him and then faced the crowd as her music changed to the introduction for another crowd favorite, her song called, *I'm a Unicorn.*

Happy and feeling safe, she stayed in-tuned with her dancers and the band. What she loved most about her shows was the band. She'd been known to have one of the best one's around. This was the life, she thought. This was her life. No one knew that behind all the glitz, glamour and bright smiles was a woman who appreciated her success but has come to realize that this wasn't all she needed.

**

He saw her. Bright and in beautiful color was Gabby on stage wowing the crowd. Adonis wanted to sit still and enjoy the performance like everyone else, but he couldn't. He had to try and not focus on Gabby and how his heart swooned just watching her perform. His body leaped with awareness as his eyes lingered on her body from her feet to the top of her beautiful head. Shaking off where his mind was going, he turned his attention from her and put it on the crowd. He analyzed as many individual people as he could set his eyes on. He was in the seat at the highest level in the arena. From this position, he could see everything. Even though the show was sold out, thanks to Jordan, he had no problem getting in.

When he arrived in Miami, he headed straight for the arena to get his pass to get inside. Giving Jordan's name, he was immediately given a five-star treatment. His pass gave him full access to every nook and cranny of the arena. He wanted to see what everyone in the arena would see. Anyone obsessed with Gabby would have purchased a ticket, probably no matter the cost, to get the best view of her. Something in him said the stalker was someone she may know. If that were the case, he wouldn't be on the front row or in the fan pit. He would be disguised and probably not enjoying the show like others. He would have his complete concentration on Gabby. He now stood at the far top in the middle of the aisle against the wall. Taking out his phone, he checked his email and was glad to see that a connect was able to get him access to Gabby's emails. It was illegal, but for him, not so much. He needed to hijack her life to see what she wasn't paying attention to. He would take a closer look later on a flight he was booked on that night to New York City.

Gabby had recently purchased a Park Avenue three-bedroom, five-bath condominium. Once Jordan sent him the address, he was able to get his hands on the floor plan. The place was laid out nice. The plans included every point of entry in and out of the building. Gabby wasn't on the top floor, but her place did have two floors. The first thing he noticed was that she needed blackout film on her windows to protect her privacy from eyes in the high-rise across from hers. He'd dive into that more, as well, when he was settled on the plane.

Adonis looked out at the stage and smiled. He caught a glimpse of Jordan dancing off to the side. He wasn't just doing the two-step moving from side-to-side. He was really going in. He looked odd standing between four security guys who were barely breathing as they scanned the crowd. He understood their assignment. He then looked for Gabby's security and found them dancing just as hard as she was. He would deal with that, hopefully, when she was ready to hear from him. He had an idea of putting a new team in place for her if she was going to continue being brazen, especially in public. Gabby was the type of woman who didn't want anyone telling her what to do. She especially wouldn't want to hear him telling her anything. If she has a list of people she would listen to, he wouldn't even be last on that list. He wouldn't be on the list at all.

His phone buzzed and this time, he was glad he remembered his noise-cancelling earbuds. Even in this rowdy crowd, he would be able to hear Trent, who was calling in.

"What's up?" he asked answering.

"What's up with you? Are you in town? I thought you were coming back today? I was expecting to see you at the shop today to see your bike. It's ready for you to speed and then get the ticket tossed out," Trent kidded.

"I've been warned by my superiors to not even think about it."

"Where are you? I hear music."

"I'm in Miami. I had to take a slight detour. I'll be home in a few days."

"Cool. Do you want your bike delivered or should I keep it here for you?"

"You can have it delivered. The property management company is there today and tomorrow getting it ready for my return. I can let Chad know you're coming. My housekeeper may be there as well to let you into the garage. If not, let me know and I'll give you the security code."

"Really? No, thank you on giving me the code. I may do something and SWAT will drop down on me out of the sky. You know how you are about security. I can have it brought by when someone is there. If you don't know the exact day you'll be home, I want you to have it in case I'm not around. Everything good? What's in Miami?"

"Gabby's concert. Jordan asked me to check things out from a security standpoint."

"You can't catch a break, huh? Work, work, work."

"It's all good. It's important. I couldn't say no."

"You wouldn't say no even if you could. It's Gabby. Is she okay?"

"Yeah, she's good. She's better than good."

"Can you just wife her already? That clown she's with isn't good enough for her. What's his name, Leonard, Lance, Lester? No, wait, it's Leotard, right?"

Adonis laughed out loud. He was happy the noise from the crowd drowned him out. He didn't want to draw attention to himself.

"His name is Leo and she can date whomever she wants."

"I know she can. Still, she's entertaining him until you get your ass together and do what I said and wife her. You know you want to. She can't hold onto that grudge until the end of time. Hey, did I tell you I love her song by the same name?

End of Time? My daughter, even at three, can't resist jumping up and rocking from side to side every time she hears it."

"It's one of my favorites too."

"I won't browbeat you too much about it. I know how sensitive you are about your feelings for her that you keep pushing back on. Why? I don't know, but it's you. Holler when you get in town and ready to hang out. I take it you'll need a few days?"

"Yeah, a few. I'll holler."

The call ended as his attention turned back to Gabby. Apparently, there was a set change happening behind her as she drew the attention to her and not the men working behind her. She does a nice job being the center of attention.

He couldn't help but think back to how her hatred for him started out different and ended so terribly. It was all his fault. To this day, she has not let up on him for not returning her love. She even wanted him to be her first. He turned that down too. He'd hurt her pride. Even if he had time for any kind of a relationship, he's not sure he would risk the only family he knew by crossing a line he saw drawn in the sand. Hearing from Jordan, perhaps he had been all wrong. Back then, Gabby had been popular. The most popular guy at her school had asked her to the prom. When she rejected his advances of what he wanted to do with her on prom night, he dropped her. He then told every guy at school who still didn't have a date to not ask her. Adonis thought he was doing a good deed stepping in. He knew Gabby had a thing for him, but he never took it seriously. Now that he has a thing for her, he doubted he could convince her that he was ready for her now.

Moving away from the wall, his eyes landed on Leo the minute he joined Gabby on stage. They would do two songs together. Then Leo would do two songs by himself while Gabby did an outfit change and took a quick break. He noticed that from other snippets of her concerts that he'd seen. He didn't like Leo. The guy was too sure of himself. He was also too hands-on with Gabby.

They easily moved into each other's arms. When the crowd thought that the two of them would kiss, as he did too, they moved away from each other. Leo spun her around and cradled her body into his body. He sang smoothly in the microphone right into her ear. Adonis fumed. The image was too much for him. He wanted to kick Leo's ass like he had done to the guy who shunned Gabby back during her prom. He felt his fists ball up as Leo's hands moved down Gabby's body. Thankfully, he didn't touch any real flesh or Adonis knew he would forget his reason for being here. He'd make a bee-line for Leo. He exhaled knowing he had no right. Gabby was not his. He had a job to do. Needing a break from the scene in front of him, he exited the main arena.

The staff saw his badge and didn't bother him as he moved about. He wanted to get a look from what Gabby would see from the stage. He made his way to the behind-the-stage area where he would climb the risers to where the camera and lighting crew from that vantage point stood. That will allow him to see who was down front. The way his neck popped, something told him that her stalker was somewhere in the crowd.

**

She was coming. He got more excited by the minute. The smartest moved he'd made was to slide a member of the venue staff two thousand dollars to allow him to borrow his uniform and badge. He could feel a rush in his brain at the idea that he was finally going to make a move on her even in a crowd. He was dressed like so many other staff that once he struck, he would then blend in. Gabby needed a quick lesson that he could get to her anytime and anywhere.

He watched Gabby leave the stage and excitedly greet her team at the bottom of the stairs. Her security wasn't paying attention, as they usually weren't. Instead, they were looking at Gabby's ass and that of the other female dancers. Now would be a great time to use the pocket knife on her and slip away without even being caught. He didn't want to hurt her but she needs to be punished for not listening to him when he said that she needed to stop letting Leo feel on her. Their display of affection repulsed and angered him. He hated it.

Getting in the midst of the crowd, he moved closer and closer until all of a sudden, a man who flashed something at everyone around her easily got her through the crowd, covering her body as he quickly moved. Panic broke out as people screamed. Her security team moved behind the man and Gabby. They didn't stop at her dressing room as he thought they would. Instead, from his spot against the wall where he was pushed in the mayhem, he saw her in all pink forced down the long hallway and out of a side door. Just like that, Gabby was gone. He missed his chance. He thought he was in the clear once he saw her brother leave the show, halfway through.

He kicked the wall behind him and ducked his head. There would be another chance. No one was going to keep him from her forever.

4

He watched her. As much as he wanted to look away, Adonis couldn't take his eyes off of Gabby. Two days ago, something horrible could have happened. He didn't know what had been planned for her. His keen sense of knowing that an abnormal change was in the air allowed him to sniff out that something was wrong. His sixth and seventh-senses had paid off.

Staying two additional days in Miami wasn't a part of his plan. Everything was clear that there were vulnerabilities everywhere when it came to Gabby. Before her Los Angeles final tour dates, he would make sure there would be no issues and no stalker. What he did to plan what may have been on his mind wasn't thwarted because he'd slipped up. Adonis' skills were the answer. He was in the right place at the right time. Thank goodness he was.

As the plane floated through the air, Adonis sat motionless in the seat across from Gabby on her private plane. She was curled up into a ball on the long butter yellow leather seat. For two days, she'd barely said anything to him. Her shock at seeing him and discovering he was rushing her of the arena still had not worn off. He didn't have a choice. On instinct, he just moved.

Gabby was angrier than he'd ever seen her before. It was all targeted at him. He took it because he had to in order to keep her safe. The silent treatment was worse than her screaming at him for hours like she had done that night.

"You're staring at me."

She was no longer sleeping. Adonis uncrossed his legs and sat straight up in his seat. Though he was exhausted having been up without sleep for several days, he was alert enough to hear the slight words she spoke. Thankfully, she hadn't raised her voice like that first night. After getting her in the truck, his driver rushed her back to her hotel, still clad in her last outfit from the show. He didn't even allow her time to go to her dressing room to change. No one stopped him when he called for his car. Just in case he would need to make a quick exit, he'd had his driver waiting with the truck running at the back entrance. He'd checked the area thoroughly and told the driver to let him know if there was anything suspicious that he could see.

"I'm watching you. There is a difference."

"Stop watching me. There is nowhere for me to go. No one can get to me thousands of feet in the air."

"You're right in front of me. What do you expect me to do?" he asked.

They were playing a cat and mouse game. He was nothing if he wasn't a winner in that field. It's what he does.

"Sit in another seat where you can't see me."

"Why? And miss the view? Not on your life."

Adonis tried to smile but then didn't. He knew this wasn't a smiling moment for her. She still hasn't forgiven him for what happened. He didn't know if that was him not being forgiven for two nights ago or eight years ago.

When she moved the blanket he'd placed over her when she'd fallen asleep about thirty minutes into the flight, she pulled her legs out from under her and placed her feet on the floor. When they first arrived on it, Gabby she sat down, pulled out a book and proceeded to ignore every effort he made to make small talk with her. It seems the standoff was over.

"You're not being funny if that's what you are attempting to do."

"I don't know. I've been told that I am good at telling a joke or two."

"Adonis, why are you here?" she finally asked.

In all of the yelling she'd been doing, this was the first time she asked him that question. He had been ready to explain everything. Somehow, in his haste to just let her have her way, he had put that to the side to keep his mind on keeping her out of harm's way.

"I'm here to help," he said.

"By somehow firing my security detail? All of them? How the hell did you do that? Who gave you the authority to do that? You had no right," she said harshly.

"It only lasts until we land in Los Angeles. I can't actually fire them. It was time to remove some of the people crowding you until a more thorough check of them could be made. I had every right to do that. If I didn't, I wouldn't have been able to do it."

"I guess this is the work of you and my brother?"

"Partly. Also, I know people."

"Right. The secret agent knows people. How come my people didn't even question when you snatched me out of there? You could have been a kidnapper for all they knew."

Adonis nodded. She's right. Thank goodness he wasn't.

"They had been told that I was someone who would have total control if anything happened. I was wearing a badge that they were told to look out for. No one was to alert you so that you would go on with your show without hesitation. You were going to be flying high in the air during your show. I didn't want you worrying and possibly falling off."

"Well, that didn't work for the last two nights. I was terrified."

"It didn't show. You were fixated on your fans. The show for all three nights that I saw was magnificent."

"I'm glad you liked it. Again, why are you here?"

"You've calmed down enough to ask me that. Are you done yelling and cursing at me?"

"I get like that when I'm mad."

"Yeah, I've been on the other end of that prior to this week."

"Adonis – stop stalling. I'm too tired to yell at you anymore. I don't want to argue. I want to know what went on that night that you felt the need to swoop in like that."

"You have a dangerous stalker," he said.

"I have a lot of stalkers. It comes with the territory."

"Your family is worried. I am worried. You should be too."

"All that because you were made aware of my stalker? That's crazy."

He needed to tell her all of it in order for her to understand.

"Gabby, this guy has access to you that is too close for comfort. Jordan was upset after a phone call you made to him the night of your first show."

"He called you and you just showed up on the second night? Just like that? Aren't you usually out of the country saving the world from terrorists or something?"

Adonis knew she was trying to be facetious, but he found it adorable.

"Humor me for a few minutes. Jordan knew I was done with my last job. I was heading home to Los Angeles for a few months of downtime, required after a long-haul deep cover assignment."

"Right, because the two of you stay in contact."

"I would have stayed in contact with you as well, but you hate me."

"With good reason," she shot back flippantly.

"I'll take that. He asked me to come look into things and I did. That night, I overheard some women saying that one of the employees suddenly came into a pocket full of cash. They were pissed that he left them to do his job. He gave them each a hundred dollars to keep quiet about it. They weren't quiet enough though, that was clear. When I checked, none of the employees were unaccounted for as far as being on the clock. One, however, had not been seen for over an hour. I took that to mean that he probably sold his place at work, possibly, to your stalker."

"Because thinking the worst that people will do is your job?"

"It is. I will never apologize for that. I don't talk about my work but the things I've seen and the people that I've stopped? I will never stop thinking of the worst in people. I take it very seriously. It's the difference between me living or dying on the job. I very much like the living part. I'm trained to notice everything."

Adonis was about to overshare. He had so much more he wanted to add to what else he has noticed. He wanted to say he loves the deep dimples on of her cheeks. They add to her intoxicating allure. Her nose piercing is sexy. He loves a woman with manicured nails, but not too long. He likes them just long enough for him to feel them scratching lightly across his back when he's... He stopped his thought. He was imagining Gabby in bed, sexily moving under him with her nails raking across his back encouraging him on with the sexy sway of her scrumptious hips.

"Did you hear me?" Gabby asked bringing him back into the conversation.

He didn't but he wouldn't admit why he heard nothing.

"What did you say?"

"I asked what happened next?"

"I assumed he was someone pretending to be on the arena staff in order to move about easily. I didn't know who but I saw a lot of the staff too close to you. That's why I pulled you out of there. Turns out, what I thought was the truth, was dead on. Yesterday, the employee was confronted and explained that he was given a couple thousand dollars to give up his uniform no questions asked. Of course, he's fired at this point. He didn't know who the guy was. He needed the money so he took it. He just thought the guy wanted to get closer to the stage where the action was."

"Oh."

In her eyes, he saw her understanding of the situation.

"I would do anything to look out for you. I wasn't trying to mess up your night or to take charge over your team. They aren't who I am; who I'm trained to be at all times. I promised Jordan."

"He has called me a million times since that night. Thankfully, the media didn't get wind of anything. To them it looked like I was in a hurry to get out of there."

"Well, that's actually the truth. It just so happens that at the time, you didn't know it."

"I guess I should say thank you instead of cussing you out and calling you all kinds of names."

"Is that part out of your system? I'm none of those things you called me."

He watched the ridges of her face soften the way they should be. The angry Gabby was someone he never wanted to see or hear from. She was too beautiful to mess up her gorgeous smile with looks of angst.

"I know and I'm sorry. I'm also thankful. What about this guy? He's starting to creep me out."

He had more to tell her but wasn't sure if she was ready to hear it yet. What he didn't want to do was lie to her. He leaned forward on his haunches.

"Listen, I need to tell you something, but I don't want you to freak out. It's about why you're on your way to Los Angeles instead of New York."

"How did you know about that?" she asked, hitting him with a questionable look. "Never mind. I'm assuming that songbird who is telling all of my business is Jordan. Tell me."

"There were cameras put in at your condo. Two in the bedroom and one in the bathroom inside of the air ventilation in the ceiling. I've got some guys on top of that right now. They'll get your condo properly secured. You have to do better. The type of protection your brothers and father have, you should know that someone will come for you if they see an opening."

Gabby covered her mouth as her eyes shot wide open.

"Oh my god! Are you serious? I haven't even really moved in there. Just my things are there. The last time I was in New York for an appearance, I stayed at a hotel because my place had been painted earlier that day."

When he watched her pull the blanket tighter around herself, he knew she was shivering through the fear of what could have been. He was horrified of the possibility that images of her in the shower could have reached social media sites.

"I need to find out who painted your place. Trust me, I'm looking into that. There is something else about your place in L.A. When was the last time you were home?"

"Months. I've been on the road for the past four months. The last time I was home, I stayed with my parents because they were in town. Why?"

Adonis paused, hoping he could avoid scaring her more than necessary. It may be unavoidable.

"Someone's been inside your L.A. condo too. Your alarm company was notified that entry had been made inside of your place at a time when you weren't home. Jordan says he knows you weren't in town because he talked to you while you were away. Somehow, someone gained entry very recently and left flowers, rose petals and other things inside, apparently to welcome you back home. There was a note left for you to that fact. Whoever this guy is, he knows everything about your whereabouts. That's where I need to start. Someone close to you is doing this. You and I will need to talk about that after I've had some rest. I've been up for three straight days. Though that's not new for me, I need to shut it down for a few days to get my clarity back."

"Okay, if all of my residences have been invaded, where am I supposed to stay since we're headed to L.A.? We'll be there in a few hours," she asked. "I do not want to stay with Jordan. I'll get a long-term stay hotel."

Adonis had another plan. It wasn't a good one and he knew it. It was the only way he knew he could keep her safe.

"Your parents are in D.C. and Jordan said your dad didn't want you at their big house by yourself. Jordan, of course, wants you to stay his house. I can take you there. A hotel isn't a good idea. I would need to have it checked thoroughly. That takes time."

"Can I stay with you? I heard you have a house in Malibu on a hill overlooking the ocean with a private beach. You're a secret agent. I bet your place has better protection, as far as a security system, than the White House. I don't want to be anywhere by myself. My family is always on the go. You already told me you're on a breather from work."

To his surprise, Gabby had read his mind. That was his solution. Common sense out the window, he was in agreement with her. Hopefully, putting her in the guest room on the first floor, an entire floor and two flights of stairs away from him would work. He was already being tested being back around her knowing she has a man. That couldn't be his concern. Her life was at stake.

"Are you sure? I don't know that I'll be any better than Jordan would be."

"You have rules? Seriously, you get that I'm a grown ass woman, right?"

"Yes, I've noticed."

He saw her about to say something else. He felt the look in his eyes change. Gabby saw it too. Somehow, she knew what he was thinking. They didn't discuss it. They left it hanging between them.

"Rules?" she asked him again.

"Don't push back on me when I tell you something is for your own good. Trust my judgement. Only one other rule. I would appreciate it if you didn't ask me why after I say it."

"Okay," she replied softly.

"No Leo on the premises. I know you're in a relationship with him. The things that lovers do, please don't. Not in my house. I can't explain it right now, but just don't. Can you handle that? Can you restrain yourself? I just need a few days to get your place looked at and get some changes made."

She nodded. He could see the wheels turning in her head.

"Then I have a rule too if I'm going to stay with you. Can you not screw any women while I'm there. I get that you're just back and all. You probably had plans for a bevy of women to flow in and out of there. I'm not sure how much, you know what, you were getting while on your case. I...can you just not?" she asked.

Adonis knew he would have no problem sticking to her rule. He didn't want any woman that wasn't her. She's not available and that was his fault. At least he wouldn't have to walk in on her lip-locked with Leo or worse, he wouldn't have to hear moans throughout his house.

"I promise I won't do that. Right now, all I need is sleep and lots of it," he admitted. As if on cue, his body replied when he let go of a huge yawn.

"If I promise to not try and runaway while on this plane, would you change places with me and get some sleep? This is the longest seat on the plane to accommodate your height comfortably."

Gabby was up and out of her seat before he could answer. He stood to switch places with her. For a moment, they stood close enough that if he leaned in a little, they would be kissing. His eyes followed her hand as she moved her long braids to the other side of her face, giving him total access to her neck if he was tempted to kiss here there. That wasn't her idea, but his – or was it?

Pulling his desire back, he moved around her to the chair. He laid down while still keeping one foot on the floor. That was a move he'd learned in his training. When not in a bed, one foot on the floor at all times to be able to feel vibrations – airplane or not.

"Thanks for the seat," he said almost on a whisper. He felt his body already relaxing and ready for a quick nap. That's all he needed to keep going a little longer until they got to his house.

"Adonis?"

Gabby calling his name, he lifted his head where he had already placed his arm across his face.

"Yeah?"

"Thanks for looking after me."

He yawned again. This time he turned his head toward the back part of the seat. As he nodded off, his mind had finally shut down as he spoke a few words before sleep overtook him.

"Anytime sweetheart," he said, and didn't know it.

**

Gabby heard it. Did he mean it? Adonis had called her sweetheart. She heard it loud and clear. The fact that she would be staying with him was already a shock to her system. She half-expected him to demand that she stay with Jordan. His reaction was almost as if he had already planned on her staying with him. She smiled when she heard him softly snoring. She'd never seen anyone drop off to sleep so fast. Being up for three days straight, she assumed would do that to a body. She didn't know. Her beauty sleep was a part of her daily regimen.

Standing, she did what he must have done when she fell asleep. She searched for a blanket to cover him. Adonis was a big man, her perfect type. He was not only the big, strong type, but he was tall, well over six feet. He was even taller than Jordan who was six-foot-three or four. There wasn't much to the blanket, but she covered as much of him as she could. He'd been taking care of her the past few days with no sleep. She loved being able to care for him even though he wasn't awake to enjoy it. She stood over him for a few moments. She took in everything about his face. There was a scar on his cheek that she didn't remember seeing years ago. There was also one that traveled his arm from his wrist all the way around to his elbow. That looked like a knife wound. Someone had cut him. That angered her. Adonis was precious to her even if she screamed at him for hours a few days ago. She was suddenly wondering how she was going to make it living a few days under the same roof as him. Here they were on a plane and all she could think about was all the man and all the meat that those clothes were hiding. She wanted nothing more than to join him by wrapping her body around his. She imagined holding onto him and never letting go. Many nights, she'd fallen asleep thinking of him and how much she still wanted to be his.

Exhaling loudly to not let her mind go there, she returned to her seat. She turned out all of the lights in the cabin, other than the small one above her head. Taking out her phone, she checked her social media pages to see what her media team had been posting for the past few days. With all of the excitement of seeing Adonis again, she completely forgot to check in with her fans.

Though there was still a crazy man on the loose after her, she already felt safe being this close to Adonis. The determination in his words and demeanor had put her at ease. She felt loved by a man who wouldn't give her his heart. How much closer they could get remained to be seen.

5

One week. That's all the time that had gone by since Adonis had brought Gabby to his house to stay temporarily. For the most part, he did what he had planned on doing. He got the sleep his body and brain reminded him that he needed. At the same time, he reached out to various people to help him get some investigative work done. He wasn't as far along as he would have liked to be, but some progress is better than no progress.

After landing from Miami, he called a call service owned by a friend of Trent's. He was assured that he would keep quiet about Gabby's presence. With her in disguise, they made their way through a private part of the airport at LAX. From there, they made a quick stop at her condo. There was no plan for her to stay but he wanted to let her get some things that she wanted to bring with her to his house. Thankfully, they had a few weeks before the shows she had coming up at the Hollywood Bowl. In the full scheme of things, that should be enough time for him to help fix her stalker situation. That was his plan. He was hoping to get some work done through his office, but that would alert his director that he wasn't following instructions. Instead, he reached out to Cypher for some information searches. Through the CIA systems, they could get a lot more done than they would if he had reached out to local authorities. He also had a few other loyal employees who would keep quiet about his requests. Things were moving on Gabby's behalf. Information was coming in daily.

As far as her security, she had a different team who looked after her in L.A. He wanted to trust them as much as she did, so he didn't disturb the work they needed to do. He did make it clear that she wouldn't be at the condo so they weren't needed unless she called for them. He didn't want a bunch of security guys near his place who he didn't trust to know what it meant to be incognito. Gabby would reach out when she had to rehearse or spend time at the studio. Times when she needed to meet with her team at her label, he would stand back and let them do their job. He also wasn't a foolish man either. He'd already called Raymond, a close friend who was a master at security. Raymond had pulled in a few other guys who helped him keep an eye on the watchers who were tasked with watching Gabby. He would see how that went to determine if he needed to pull those guys too while keeping Ray in place.

So far, there had been checks into some of the people closest to Gabby. He needed to get a more complete list, something he was working on. Gabby was helping some, but he knew that she was getting frustrated feeling like she was a prisoner in his home. They were pretty much living two separate lives unless he needed to get information from her about the people she called, *her people.*

The first two days, she loved being at the house and down on the beach. He discovered easily that Gabby was the ultimate party girl. She was used to being a big part of the L.A. scene. Now wasn't the time to be out and about until he could get further in the investigation. She was getting antsy and it was showing in her responses to him. Her answers were becoming short and curt. Just this morning, she snapped at him for not having grapes in the house, something she wanted. When she wanted to go to her condo to get her Range Rover so that she could feel like she had a little more freedom to move about, he told her how he thought it was a bad idea. Everyone knew that Range Rover and knew it was her. He offered to go get what she needed or to have his housekeeper do it. She kept his place stocked with all kinds of food. She would pick up anything by request. Nothing appeased Gabby. Bottom line was, she wanted out of his house. She didn't respond to his counter offer. Instead, she stormed off and slammed the door to her bedroom. He stood for a few minutes with his eyes on her door. He didn't like how the conversation ended. If by chance, she wanted to take a few minutes to calm down and come back out, he would be there waiting. She didn't. He went into his home gym and worked out. Exerting energy helped to keep his mind fresh. With Gabby around and his promise to not have other women in the house, he was frustrated beyond belief.

Hours later, he was dressed and about to head out. When he came down the steps from his bedroom, she came from around a corner and stopped right in front of him.

"You're going out?" she asked.

"I am."

"Can I go? I'm tired of being in here. This sitting here doing nothing is boring."

"Gabby, it won't be like this always. This house is secluded for a reason. It's to give me my privacy and some peace and quiet," he explained.

"You live like a monk. That surprises me. I thought that since you've been away for so long that you would come home and hit the club scene with your friends. I see them coming by and calling. You're not itching to go out?"

Moving around her to go into the kitchen, he tried to come up with the words to once again explain to her what his version of respite was.

"No, I'm not itching to be out in a crowd with a bunch of sweaty, drunk people. That's not my thing. If I'm going to be covered in sweat, I'm good doing that here at home."

Adonis didn't think about the words he said until they left his mouth. He was definitely sexually frustrated. Without thinking, he said things that made him think of sex."

"I bet you do," Gabby said.

He ignored her snide remark. He knew what she meant.

"I've learned to enjoy being still. You should try it instead of complaining as if I'm keeping you hostage."

"What would you call this? I'm in this house with no transportation. Not even my bike. I need to get my exercise."

"I have an entire gym in my house. You can do all the working out you need to get done."

"There has been nothing from this stalker guy. I think he's tired of the chase and has moved onto someone else. That's my guess. I need to get out and party with my friends. People expect me to get out and be seen. I draw in the crowds to the clubs. It's how I connect with my fans."

After grabbing a bottle of water, he turned to face her after taking a big gulp.

"You're talking about Leo, right? Is that the friend you're talking about? I'm keeping you from him?"

"Jealous?" she shot out at him harshly.

"Hell no. Do you and have fun doing it," he replied.

"I would but I'm on lockdown like some two-year-old."

"I'm not locking you down. I just want you to be more selective about your choices. Don't forget there is always going to be some kind of threat to you out there. Right now, there is a real one. This is not a joke."

"Ugh, holding me in this house is. What about when I need to get to rehearsal next week? I'm working on new songs. I need to get to the studio."

"Then go. You can call your team to pick you up and drop you back off here."

"Is my place ready yet?"

"Why? Am I that hard to live with that you're ready to leave? Your condo board has agreed to make some much-needed security upgrades to the building from my suggestions and Jordan's recommendations. I'm working on the ones for your unit specifically."

"Whatever. Where are you running off to?"

"I'm meeting a friend."

"Friend? A woman friend? I guess I'm not the only one in this house who needs some human contact."

"Gabby, stop. That's not what this is. Besides, you and I are having human contact."

"Barely. You've been avoiding me. Do you always spend that much time upstairs in your room? You spend a lot of time out on your patio that's connected to your bedroom? I can see you out there when I'm down on the beach. I feel like you're doing things like staying in your room to avoid being near me.

Am I still that toxic as far as you're concerned? I know how much I repulsed you years ago. I see that hasn't changed."

"Whoa, where is this coming from? I've never been repulsed by you."

"Are you going out to see a woman? Are you coming back tonight or will I be in this big ass house alone? You know what, forget I even asked. I am going out tonight. Enough of this. If you can go out, I can go out."

Adonis didn't want to tell her that he'd called Cypher who had taken a flight into L.A. to meet with him. They were making a little progress and were thinking that the threat was actually someone in her own camp. He needed more information before telling her that. He was meeting up with him later in the evening.

"Like I said, you're not being held hostage. Go where you like. I guess you're going to make plans with Leo? That's cute," he said, sounding dismissive.

He knew what his tone relayed and he didn't care. The moment Gabby said she was going out, his mind went straight to her and Leo and what they could get into.

"Why do you care? At least he lets me know that I'm not a toad."

"Gabby, I've never, ever said anything like that. I've also never thought that."

"What's wrong with me? I know you've been with women. I just want to know why you never thought about me that way?"

He didn't know what to say. He looked into her eyes and saw a world of hurt. He wanted to take that hurt away, but he was afraid of what that could lead to with them under one roof.

He'd been struggling every night being one floor away from her. He wanted her like he wanted and needed his next breath. The truth was, he was going out to get some space between them. The night before, he almost crept downstairs because after a week of having her in his house, his body was overriding his common-sense of staying away from her. She had to stay off-limits to him. He knew what Jordan said, but still, he didn't want to mishandle her. Besides, she was so into Leo that he found it sickening. That feeling was all mixed up in jealousy too.

"No, Gabby. We're not going there. Nothing is wrong with you and you know it. Several times, you've been named the most beautiful girl in the world. Do not try to play victim with me when it comes to how you look."

She rolled her eyes and moved away from the kitchen counter. Alone. By herself. Without him. Adonis' mind was racing with lust. He didn't know what he would do if she went out to see Leo tonight. He needed space. She was looking up at him and all he wanted to do was pull her into his arms and kiss her until they needed to breathe. He wouldn't let her go. He would make love to her mouth the way in which his body was screaming to do with hers. He couldn't. This was Gabby. He had to remember that.

He needed to leave. He had a few things he needed to do. She was tired of being in the house after a week. He was tired of fighting the struggle within.

"Go be all dark and mysterious. I hope the woman you're going to see has the *time* of her *life*. I'm going to take a hot shower and make plans for tonight. Leo called about me joining him at an appearance we were already scheduled to make. I was going to pass, but now, I think I'll go. This ass needs music!"

Adonis started to object as if he had a choice. Instead, he moved out of her way to let her go by him. Without saying another word, he grabbed his keys and rushed to the garage. In less than a minute, he was in his truck and out of the garage. Withing seconds, he was speeding down Pacific Coast Highway. Perhaps, when he got back, they could have a serious talk. He wasn't ready yet. He needed a moment.

**

Gabby danced around the bedroom while she completed her look for the night. She'd called Leo so that he could swoop by and pick her up for their stop at two clubs tonight. As usual, they were being paid handsomely to come by and show their faces. All day on every social platform imaginable, word had been going around that fans could catch her and Leo in the VIP section of both clubs. The hype was real as she read some of the social media posts from fans who couldn't wait to see the sexiest couple alive make an appearance.

After touching up her makeup, she turned the music down, grabbed a small bag and took one last look at herself in a barely-there tiny black dress. It hugged her perfect curves everywhere. She'd also spoken with Victoria who was making plans to visit her. To hear that made her day. Since Adonis was acting as if they were strangers, she could use a friendly face and even friendlier company. She tossed an imaginary middle finger up at Adonis. She didn't mean it. She felt good getting a little frustration off of her chest.

She had all but forgotten the argument that was close to taking place with Adonis earlier in the day. She'd touched base with a few of her friends without telling them where she was staying. On that, she did listen to Adonis when he told her to keep her whereabouts as quiet as possible. He joked about not wanting to shoot any of her friends caught sneaking around. She got it.

Several of her friends told her that a game was circulating around social with everyone trying to guess where she was. No one could believe that she hadn't hit up any clubs in a week. That was her thing and she missed it. She was out of this house tonight even if it killed her. Then she thought about the words that came out of her mouth. Making a joke about being killed was not the best choice of thoughts.

Turning everything off in her room, she went out knowing Leo's team would be there any minute to pick her up. She promised Adonis that Leo wouldn't come in his house or spend that night, but he didn't say anything about him picking her up. He was the only person she shared her location with.

Before she could get too far, she looked up and Adonis was standing in the kitchen. The scene was reminiscent of their earlier encounter. This time, she knew she looked a lot different; definitely a lot better than being in her casual yoga pants and t-shirt. Eat your heart out, Adonis, she thought to herself when she saw how his eyes bulged out when he saw her.

"I guess you are going out. Nice material for what should be a dress."

As much as she wanted to shoot back with something smart-ass-like or sinister, she let him have that. He isn't the first jealous man to say that and he won't be the last. She had a killer body meant for dresses like this. She knew she was wearing the hell out of it.

"I won't dignify that with any sort of answer. Mainly because, again, grown-ass woman status happening in this space right here," she explained, pointing to herself. "I don't owe you an explanation for anything I do."

"I guess Leo is in the limo I see on the camera sitting outside."

"Yes."

"Coming back tonight? I don't see an overnight bag."

Gabby looked him up and down.

"Expend any condoms while you were out?"

"Really?" he questioned.

"Don't start nothing and there won't be anything. For every smart remark you have, I have an even smarter answer."

"I hope in all that you and Leo get into tonight that you remember to make sure his security team is watching out for you."

Gabby started to walk toward the garage when she turned back around. She couldn't let this go.

"Is that all that matters to you? Keeping me alive and whether or not I'm going to be spending the night with Leo?"

"Inquiring minds want to know whether to expect you back tonight or not."

He lied, but honesty would make him look like a fool.

"You don't have a right to question anything about me. None!" she yelled. "Do you know how good it feels to have someone appreciate and want you? On the other hand, do you have any idea what it's like to be rejected by someone you have the deepest love for...had the deepest love for? No, I bet you don't. See, you're Adonis and your name alone makes you irresistible to women. You welcome me into your house but you don't want me to see the one man in my life who looks at me and sees a woman and not a little fifteen or even an eighteen-year-old girl. At least he doesn't hide behind the past. You and I both know what you see when you look at me in the present. Stop treating me like I'm insignificant to you. Stop it or take me home and leave me there. Don't have me here and then say things about how I'm dressed as if I'm not sexy as hell! Again, jealous much? Don't answer. I already know the answer. I think it's time for me to go home or maybe to a hotel until my place is ready. I don't know how much longer I can take the looks and the stares. The criticism like you're my man is getting old. I can read your eyes. They don't match your mouth. I can take care of myself out in *these* streets."

"If you could, you wouldn't be here. I wouldn't have needed to be a presence in Miami. The streets are crazy. Do you not fully understand *that*?"

"Oh, I understand a lot of things. Stop hiding behind that. I know the look of a man who wants me. You'll never admit it and that's okay, but don't treat me like I'm stupid. I understand the threat. It will always be there. Do you know what won't always be here? Me! I won't always be *here*. I'm going out tonight to have some fun. Feel free to put the alarm on. I know the code if I decide to come back here tonight. If not, I'll see you in the morning. Hopefully by then, you'll have some news about my place. I'm sick of being here. I'm sick of you avoiding me. I'm sick of excuses in place of what you really want to say. I'm just sick of it. I'll let you go back to your existence, whatever that looks like for you. Don't ask me to keep staying here with a front row seat to the version of Adonis who still treats me like a kid. *Look* at me! I'm a woman, dammit! Do you see me? Do you? Bye Adonis. I'm out. Have fun in this lonely existence of yours. Don't try to put me down because I want to be around people who really want me around."

Gabby didn't give Adonis time to say anything. She rushed out, slamming the garage door on her way out. She rushed to the limousine and got in. She shook off her encounter with Adonis and focused on the night ahead of her.

"Hey cutie! Who lives here? This house is everything!" Leo exclaimed.

"A friend of my family. Nobody important. Are you ready to do this? Fans are waiting."

Leo leaned over in her direction, close to her ear.

"You look hot! Sexier than any woman I've ever been this close to. I think tonight, we should talk about a more solidified relationship. It's time, baby."

"Here you go. Not right now. Let me get a few drinks in me. I have been cooped up for a week. I don't want to hear anything that's not music," she said.

She looked over and smiled back at him. She looked over to the house as the garage door went down. Adonis must have closed it behind her. She was angry that she forgot. She had been forgetting a lot of things lately, like herself and what she wanted. Maybe it was time she considered giving Leo a little more of her time and attention. He's been doing all kinds of things to please her lately. Why not? She considered the possibility as the limo pulled away from the house to take them to their first club of the night. She'd wasted enough time on Adonis. She was ready for whatever the night would bring as she leaned back into the leather of the limo. Leo handed her a glass of champagne. She was ready to get the party started a little early. With Leo's arm now draped across her shoulder, maybe tonight, she would end her night in a different bed than the one she kept waking up in all alone. To her, that was the never-ending, coldest moment of her existence.

6

Adonis laid his pool cue across the pool table. Shaking his head in disgust at himself, he reached into his back pocket to pull out his wallet. He shouldn't be surprised that he had again lost another game of pool to his partner in crime, Cypher. In public, he never used his given name, only his CIA code name. He himself had never been called by his real name by those he worked with. They were required to never compromise who they were by speaking their government names.

After tossing a one-hundred-dollar bill across the table, he and Cypher headed back to their table in the corner. The waitress walked up to them carrying two massive bacon cheeseburgers, fries and beers. He was thankful for the distraction from thinking about Gabby and what she could be doing right now.

"Man, one day you'll stop challenging me to pool," Cypher chortled.

Adonis expected him to make fun of the way their games often turned out. Adonis lost every single time.

It wasn't often that they had a chance to connect outside of work. Adonis called on his friend in his time of need. Keeping Gabby safe was the neediest he's ever been outside of work.

"I'm going to keep trying. I am persistent. I will beat you at pool one day. I know you got your pool skills from your days of growing up in Baltimore. I didn't play much pool until I met you. I'm on the rise though. Watch your back!" Adonis cheered.

"How did you find this place? It's sort of off the beaten path."

"And it's black-owned."

"I just bit into a sweet potato fry and I can tell that someone's grandma is in that kitchen seasoning this up!"

"I love coming here. It's one of my favorite places when I'm home. I try to make my rounds to support the small businesses when I can. Places like this help relax me when I'm coming down from the high of a mission."

"You were pretty deep cover on your last Op. How are you handling it? How's the quiet? How's the lack of adrenaline flow that's usually amped up when you're on a mission? I know there hasn't been a lot of time that has passed since we last talked. Just checking in on you."

Instead of scanning the crowd in the bar as he usually does out of habit, Adonis looked down at the beer in his hand. Now that he has the burger, he was contemplating if he still wanted what he ordered. Eating was the furthest thing from his mind.

"Having this time to decompress should be a good thing for me, but it's not. Something personal has me on edge, hence the call to you. I will say, you didn't have to fly all the way here. I needed some insight into the situation around what's happening to Gabby. I can't get her to take it seriously. That bothers me and it bothers her family."

"The politician. His family, right?"

Adonis nodded. That was the name he'd always called Jordan since they were back in high school together. He always had a legal mind, even as a youngster. Some teased him for being uppity and uptight while he admired Jordan's desire to be something. Him being the son of a staunch politician, it was only logical that Jordan would pick up his own desire for that field.

"Yeah, that's them."

"And Gabby is? Are you admitting anything to yourself yet?" Cypher asked.

Adonis started to speak but didn't. He simply looked toward his friend and Cypher already knew. When he nodded, Adonis knew that the unspoken words were louder than any his friend could have said out loud.

"You know."

"I have a Gabby type of woman in my life," Cypher admitted.

"Is that so? What is a Gabby type of woman?" Adonis questioned.

"She is the woman that you know is the most perfect specimen that God has ever created. You also know that she's your one and only. Either you're fighting it or she is. For me, she fights me all the way. I've done everything in my power to let her know that she means everything to me; that I'd turn the world upside down just for her. She's afraid of feeling like that for anyone, especially any man. If I didn't know her history, I would have walked away. I do know her past. I know what she's been through. It makes me love her and want to have her even more. I keep letting her tear me down, tear me apart and still, no other woman has ever gotten under my skin the way that she has."

"I'm definitely the opposite of that spectrum from where you are, but I'm still on the same field. I have always avoided, what I considered, a childhood crush. I was good until I stepped up as her knight and shining armor one day back when she was eighteen. I stomped all on her heart by not returning the affection she had for me. She was too young for me. Her brother was and still is my best friend. Her family embraced me as one of them. I came from a rough part of Compton. Most of the people from my neighborhood barely made it out of middle or high school. College was a mystery. Back then, their father was Governor of California. You and I had similar upbringings, so I know you understand. We were recruited under the same guise – on a life track that would have landed us in prison or the graveyard. I was given a last chance in a program he had established. That not only took me out of Compton, where no one missed me, but brought me to Calabasas. Through Jordan's family, I met and connected with some amazing people who challenged me. That was a world I didn't know existed. They took me in, helped me secure a better education and put me on the road to where I am now. I felt like I would be betraying them if I got involved with Gabby."

"So, you joined the agency, like me, and you left your heart behind. You lied to her and yourself. Now, fast-forward to the present and she still hates you for what, leaving her? Yet you now realize how much you love her. Am I close?" Cypher garnered and questioned with a raised eye-brow.

"You've seen pictures and videos of her. She's not only gorgeous as hell, but there is a light in her that I'm drawn to. I didn't know it until this time when I returned because her

72

brother called me for help. As I told you when we spoke, someone is terrorizing her. Those checks into people's lives are all about her. Whoever it is knows a lot about her. This guy knows things, people and places pertaining to her that would not easily be found. Sure, she's a star with a fanbase of millions along with the income to match. She's a target. She's hot, sexy – just downright gorgeous. Any man would be lucky to have her. Whoever this person is, he wants her by any means necessary. I think he's borderline on the verge of being willing to take her life just to be sure no other man has her. You know how we are; everyone is suspect."

"I understand. I'm on my way to Baltimore because the woman I spoke of has a family that could be in danger and she doesn't know it. I'm hoping to get there to fix things before peril reaches across the globe to where she was able to escape to. Thankfully, she's been able to avoid the mayhem that is life in Baltimore. I would risk it all just to keep her from harm. I know that's where you are too or you wouldn't have called me. What else do you need? I only hit on the surface based on what you asked for."

Adonis placed his beer back down on the table and rubbed his temples with his middle fingers. After swiping his hand down his face to and through his full beard, he was ready to put it all on the line.

"I need a deeper dive into those who are closest to Gabby. Either this threat is coming from someone in her camp or someone close to her is giving out information. Perhaps through a payoff of some type. I had to whisk her out of Miami and back here. The biggest thing is, before she landed, I had a few guys go over and check her place out. Someone had been inside of her condos. I was surprised that her current security detail didn't note vulnerabilities all around the place here in town. She can't continue to live like an everyday person. She has thousands of fans scrabbling for her attention. Every one of her shows are sold out. She performs in some of the largest concert venues in the country. I don't think Gabby realizes how famous she is. She's reckless and it could get her hurt or killed. Either of those things would kill everything good that's left inside of me."

"What's the latest now?" Cypher asked, sitting up straight. Adonis knew he and Cypher had something in common. They often struck up conversations that brought up their similar backgrounds. Now they have a lot in common when it came to their personal lives.

"I'm glad you called to tell me you were here. I was shocked but not surprised. She thinks I'm trying to keep her as a prisoner. She's able to strong-arm everyone else they put in place to look after her. When I tell you, she is strong-minded, strong-willed and determined to do what she wants when she wants. She doesn't consider what can happen with the slightest mistake or error in judgement. She romps around like she's not a celebrity. She thinks she can walk out, get in her car and head to a store to shop like she won't get mobbed."

"What happened at the condo issue? You mentioned she isn't staying there?"

Adonis knew he had to come clean. He looked away as he prepared to respond, not wanting to see the look on his friend's face.

"Man, I'm stupid. Before I tell you, just keep in mind, I know I didn't make the right move."

"What did you do? Wait, don't tell me she's staying with you."

Adonis dropped his head and nodded slightly. He couldn't even get the words out himself.

"She's been at my house for the past week and giving me hell every single day. She's on this independent woman kick. She reminds me every moment of the day that she can do whatever she wants and that it's her life. She's a walking powerhouse. She thinks this person who is sending her these notes, emails, menacing gifts and all, is just a fan. She thinks it's what happens to all celebrities. That may be the case, but this is different. It may even be someone she's been involved with before."

"Involved with? As in relationship? We can get a deep background done on them all. I guess that's where I come in," Cypher offered. "You need more which requires my level of clearance. I'm sure you can't use yours because you aren't supposed to be doing anything work-wise.

"Exactly. You know how the director is. If I touch anything, I'll be flagged. I don't trust anyone to look into this without alerting the powers that be that they're doing it for me. I need help looking into lives in a way that we would when it comes to an operative. I know I'm asking a lot. She's fighting me because she's still hurt. I didn't think it was possible for her to still feel this way, especially since she's involved with someone now."

"Oh? Who?"

"Leo Frank."

"The crooner? What I've seen about them is true? Really? Damn! He's as big of a star as she is. He's also known for being a womanizer. Your woman is about that life with him?"

Adonis felt his fingers stiffen along with his spine. He hated even thinking about what Gabby and Leo were doing, especially tonight.

"She is out tonight. It's been all over every social media site. It's not hard to find her. Seeing her locking hands and arms with him is self-torture. Nah, I'm not about that kind of life for myself."

"In other words, you're jealous. Why don't you come clean with her about your true feelings?"

"I think it's too late for that. Besides, like I said, she's seeing someone. She's already pissed that being at my house is impacting her personal life. She called it her sexy, dating life."

"Jaguar, she's trying to get under your skin."

"It worked. I'm out here playing pool because I couldn't stand being in that house simmering over what she's doing tonight outside of what social media shows."

"Don't do that to yourself. Stay focused so you don't lose focus on why someone is coming for her. You know what can happen if you don't stay on point. You know what information I need. Get that to me and I'll get my best people going a few steps further in the checks – not just the usual surface stuff that I've been gathering. In the meantime, let's stick together on this. Keep your head in the game. I will say this, Leo or no Leo, I bet if you talk to her, really talk to her, you'll find that nothing is too late. If she's coming at you with anger all the time, it's because her childhood crush on you has turned into a woman still in love. With you now feeling the same way and the two of you under the same roof, one of two things will happen. She'll continue to resent you for the past and fight you. Or you'll forget the purpose of all of this. That's when you'll allow the images that I know are racing through your mind of her with Leo or maybe the next man, diminish your capacity to stay on task. Don't forget your training because your heart is involved. I'm doing my best to take my own advice, trust me. It's a dangerous struggle. Talk to her and clear the air so that you can handle her with the kind of care she needs. You can't hold back and allow her to walk through this situation like it's not a dire one. You won't live with yourself if anything happens to her because you're giving her grace out of your love for her."

"I know you're right. That's why I reached out to you."

"We are trained to always reach to each other when we're feeling out of sorts. It's how we pull ourselves back from the ledge. I'm taking a military flight back east. Send me what you know and I'm on it. I don't know Gabby, but I do know you. We've never talked about another woman who has gotten this close to you. She's special. Don't let that go. Again, Leo or no Leo, sounds to me like you and Gabby need to talk and either work this out or sweat it out. Pick one because without either, you're going to be stuck on this merry-go-round."

"I got you. Now that we've done a dive into my personal life, let me hear about your woman. We've touched on her a time or two, but if you're heading to Baltimore on a mission to save her family, a place I know you'd like to forget about, she must be something."

"You have no idea. I have been in love with her since we were teenagers. Her name is, get this – it's her given name; her name is *Amerikka*. It's sounds the same, but spelled different. From day one, she's had my heart. I only wish that she would let me in to show her that I would take great care of hers."

"Look at us – special agents who have the ability to take down the world's most dangerous criminals but we can't get our love lives in check," Adonis joked.

"Yeah, we're a pair. You've been open about your lady. Let me tell you about mine."

Adonis was already feeling better knowing that Cypher would be on the case, going places with it that he dares not go.

He picked up his burger and bit into all the deliciousness he remembered about it. He had an appetite again. He pushed out of his mind the argument he and Gabby had before she left his house to meet up with Leo. Despite her not wanting him to hover, he had every plan in mind to continue doing so. More than that, it was time this was also about a life he'd like to have with her; that is, if her love for him was still a possibility. He could only hope that keeping her at bay didn't turn her off from him completely.

7

Gabby removed her shoes the moment she entered Adonis' beachfront house. It was the middle of the night and her high-heels would definitely click loudly as she walked across the floor to the first-floor guestroom where she was staying. The fact that she came back to his house when she could have gone home to her own place against his wishes for her spoke to how much she loved being here. She wouldn't tell him that. For years, she had longed to be in his presence. Now, she was close to him, just not as close as her heart reminded her that she wanted to be.

Pulling slightly on the little black dress that hugged her body like a glove over all of her mountainous curves, she could feel it slipping back up to just below her behind. From the lighted entrance that turned on the minute she opened the door from the garage, she looked down into her deep cleavage and tried to also pull the dress up. If it wasn't for the large size of her natural breasts, she would have loved to go out without the removable dress straps. The crowd she knew she and Leo would be in could have been an accident waiting to happen if a fan was able to reach out for her, snatching her dress down.

That had almost happened to her once before. She remembered that lesson.

Running her hand through her long black tresses, she shook her hair out looking forward to getting a tie to pull it up on top of her head. Thankfully, the air conditioning was on in the house, giving her reprieve from the heat of the summer night. She hated that it was still ninety degrees at two in the morning. To her surprise, exhaustion fused through her. The house seemed quiet. She wondered where Adonis was.

The house was dark and mysterious just like him. She could hear the waves crashing against the rocks below the house as she walked toward the kitchen. She stopped suddenly when a possible reality came to mind. When she entered the house, she had to turn off the alarm by entering the code Adonis gave to her. If the alarm was on, that could mean that he wasn't home. Though his truck was in the garage alongside his motorcycle, she knew he also had a car that wasn't in its usual spot in front of the garage. He must be out. What if he was with a woman? She was jealous at the idea of it. Serves her right, she thought as she walked into the kitchen before heading to her room. Was he expecting her to come back or did he think their argument would have her returning to her own home or possibly to Leo's place? She'd already told him that she preferred to be at her own place and not here. She had lied. Instead, she was in his home, tiptoeing and about to grab a big bowl of the shrimp salad he'd made her earlier. Being mean, she had refused to eat because she was being child-like. Why couldn't she just admit that she still loved him like crazy? Why did she have to leave his house planting the seed in the atmosphere that she couldn't wait to get to a real man like Leo who didn't have a problem showing and telling her his true feelings? Why had she lied? Adonis made her so mad hopping back into her life for the sole purpose of rescuing her. Why couldn't he just love her like she wanted him to?

Not once had she forgotten about him in eight years. Not a single night went by without her wishing she was in his arms. She wrecked her own psyche imagining the women who were in his arms and in his bed, two places she wanted to be. Why did he have to still be so damn fine? Why couldn't she let go of the love she'd had for him since day-one?

Placing her bag on the marble countertop, she reached for the refrigerator door and smiled when she saw the long pan of shrimp salad. How did he remember that this was still her favorite pig-out food? The idea took her back to the early years being at home where her family would have big cookouts. Adonis would always volunteer to whip up some good food. Kudos, she thought, to whoever taught him how to cook. He was a master at it. To her, he was a master at everything. There were a few things she would like to know first-hand if he was a master at. They'd never crossed that line, though she very much wanted to.

Taking out the pan, she placed it on the counter without turning on any lights. What was missing were crackers to eat with the salad. She started opening cabinets to find some. If he made the salad for her, he surely would not have forgotten that crucial part of her perfect snack. She opened one cabinet after another and found nothing.

"They're in the pantry."

Gabby almost jumped out of her skin at the husky sound of Adonis' deep voice. Her body snapped around and followed the sound of his voice.

"Are you out of your mind?" she yelled. "You scared me to death."

Gabby worked to calm her heavy, loud breathing.

"Sorry. I didn't mean to scare you. I didn't want you to turn around and see a shadow sitting here. I didn't know how else to let you know I was here other than to say something."

"Why the hell are you sitting there in the dark like a stalker? Are you insane scaring me like that?" she asked, doubling over in order to catch her breath.

"A stalker in the dark in my own home? I love sitting here looking out at the ocean this time of night, or early morning, depending on how you see it. Which would you call it by the way you are tipping around at this hour?"

She could hear the humor in his voice, but she wasn't laughing. She was genuinely scared. At the same time, she was happy he was home. She could erase the image of him with a woman at this hour. Shamefully, she wasn't bothered that the very image she didn't want of him with a woman, she'd left with him of her with Leo. Little did he know that she actually loathed Leo with everything in her.

"I wasn't tipping," she replied, walking into the pantry to search for the perfect cracker. This time she did turn on a light. The pantry was like a small bedroom it was so large. With an assortment of crackers to choose from, she found her favorite and grabbed the entire box.

"Gabby, you took your shoes off before entering. I'm sitting right here. I actually saw you tipping like a thief in the night. It's all good. Hungry?"

"Starving. Mind if I eat some of your shrimp salad?"

"If I wasn't sitting here, wouldn't you have eaten it anyway? Why ask?"

"Because you're sitting there."

"What's mine is yours in this house. When I told you that the first day you arrived, I meant it; I still do. Eat away. Leo didn't feed you? You've been out with him for hours and you're starving? Or was it not that kind of date? You know, the kind where you eat food?"

Gabby was seething. She didn't like what he was insinuating.

"Why are you worried about the kind of date I was on? You somehow keep forgetting that I'm a..."

"Yes, I know – you're a grown ass woman. You love reminding me of that," Adonis said, interrupting her usual rant.

"Like always, you can't seem to remember that."

"I know who I see when I look at you. I see a woman. I also see a woman who is irresponsible and wild in her choices of men and activities. I heard that there was almost a stampede in the club once you and Leo arrived. I'm glad they were able to whisk you both to VIP before that happened. I guess that's the life of a sexy power couple, huh? You should have had your team in place. You need to let me get my team in place for you. Your guys are terrible anyway. I thought the ones in Miami were bad. Where are you getting these poorly trained bodyguards?"

"They are paid by my record label. I'm still alive without your help or the help of your mercenary looking guys. I'm good. Stop treating me like I need a babysitter. You don't have privileges with me to that extent," she shot back.

"What? I need to have privileges to care about you? To want to protect your life from a crazed person whom you seem

83

to shove to the back of your mind? One of us needs to be thinking with a level head."

"You're always the level-headed thinker, right? You always make the right decisions. You're perfect that way."

"Gabby, I'm not trying to fight with you again. This is pointless. I worry about you. I am concerned about how your night went and what could have happened. Your team is too busy looking at you in your latest shorty-short dress to really look out for what's around you."

"Oh, now it's my dress! You are relentless. There is so much about my life that you detest. Why am I here? If you would like for me to go home so that you don't have to be exposed to the choices I make for myself, which I'm free to do, just say so. I didn't ask for any of this. I can stay with Jordan if my home isn't safe."

"I have someone who is working on the security at your condo. It should be locked up tight tomorrow. You'll be good after that."

Her ego instantly deflated. Adonis had people working hard to get her out of his hair as soon as possible. She didn't want that. She wanted him to want her. She wanted him to want her to still stay with him even if there was no reason too. The fact that she hadn't thanked him for all that he was doing showed to how selfish she was still being.

She opened the refrigerator again to get extra mayonnaise. She needed her back to him so that when she asked her next question, the look on his face and his response wouldn't show the hurt on her face. He cut the light in the room on and a soft glow covered the kitchen and the large sun room where he sat near a window. She knew that where he sat was also one of her favorite places to sit in his home. The view was unlike anything she'd ever seen. The few times she'd sat there alone, there was a peace that emitted from the view that she'd never seen before.

"You want me to leave that bad? I guess you've perfected how to make me feel like an ugly duckling. I'm not surprised."

Gabby closed her eyes wishing she could take those words back. She sounded like that same eighteen-year-old wounded girl.

"Is that what you think?" he asked her.

"It's what I know."

"No, it's what you assume; you don't know. You have no idea."

"If you say so. We keep having these repeat conversations that end in me storming out like earlier. I'm hungry and I don't feel like fighting with you."

"We're talking, not fighting."

"You're trying to have total control over me and what I say and how I react. I don't like it."

"What you don't like is me. Admit it. It's not what I do, but what I haven't done. You know damn well that everything I'm doing is for your protection. I would give my life for you."

That last part, she heard him say it but his voice grew softer. She softened her tone too.

"I'm not asking you to give your life for me," she replied.

"I'm trying to explain to you that you don't have to. Do you know anyone outside of your family who would say they would give their life for you? I would die for you. That's how much I care about you. Someone is out to hurt you. I know what a terrible outcome that could be. You have no idea what I encounter every day when I'm on the job. People who walk through life thinking they are untouchable are the ones who end up dead. Even when I have to question the good or the bad, I have to lean to the bad in order to be sure I'm thinking clearly. I see danger where some people don't think to look. I'm trying to make sure if no one else is looking at the seriousness of what's happening, I will. If that makes me the villain who produces, directs and stars in your dreams, I'll take it. I'm trying my best to protect you. You're trying to punish me for my past wrongs against you. Something has to give."

Gabby turned around and their eyes locked. His voice sounded like he was pleading with her. There was something in his piercing, coal black eyes that warmed her. She hadn't looked at him this long or penetratingly in years. There was something new in his eyes. She huffed and let go of the tension that was feeding the moment.

"I get it. You said past wrongs. You did something wrong in the past?" she asked.

"I hurt you. Isn't that what all this aggression is still about? I apologize if I'm barking up the wrong tree here. Every single time over the past eight years that we've encountered each other you have frozen me out. Are you ever going to forgive me for turning you down that night?"

There it was. For the first time since back then, Adonis is broaching the subject that's been taboo for them. She has never had a chance to talk about it to anyone other than Victoria, Sierra and her mother. The only person who knows the true depth of her hurt is her mother. They shared everything, especially where she went wrong in not being the kind of woman Adonis could see himself with. She'd made a fool of herself handing him a condom while at her prom. What followed was her greatest embarrassment. That was when she decided to focus on her career and not a man.

"It wasn't just about that night," she admitted.

"It was about me belittling your feelings, right? I didn't mean to do that."

"I felt ugly and unwanted. Every boy I encountered wanted me; all of them. I know what I look like. That's not ego – it's fact. To me, in your eyes, the beautiful person I saw in the mirror somehow seemed tainted in your eyes as far as I was concerned. That hurt."

Gabby leaned back against the refrigerator door as Adonis stood and walked toward her. She eyed him in knee-length, loose fitting black basketball shorts and a white tank top. Goodness, she thought. All she saw were muscles on top of muscles bulging out everywhere. His arms, above the elbows were tatted up. Her favorite tattoo on him was of a Jaguar across the side of his neck. Oh, how she loved a man with tattoos. She had one on her lower back of a bouquet of purple roses. Perhaps one day, they could scope out each other's art. Her mind drifted.

Adonis came around the counter and stood opposite her.

"Let's have this out right here and right now. It's beyond time that we talk about what happened back then."

"I don't want to. I can't go back to the feelings that I felt back then."

She turned her head away from him, unable to hold his gaze. The more he looked at her the way he was doing now, the more she still wanted him; the more she loved him. She wouldn't do that again. She wouldn't fall back into those feelings only to be rejected again.

"Look at me, please," Adonis pleaded.

She sniffled. He had to have heard her. Gabby surprised herself that the sound of her doing so was so loud. She hated being this embarrassed in front of him. She couldn't do it. Gabby knew she wasn't strong enough.

"Why?" she uttered softly.

"Please?" he quickly asked.

She then turned and met his gaze.

"I have regretted how I handled that night and your feelings. I treaded on them like they weren't serious. You were eighteen, I was twenty-three. There was so much at stake. You are not an ugly anything. You are strikingly beautiful. You always have been. You have grown even more beautiful with time. It's not just the star-studded beauty that comes with what a celebrity can do to look good. You are a natural beauty. I saw it back then and I still see and recognize it now. I did you wrong and I am sorry. I am *so sorry*. I never, ever meant to hurt you. I... I..."

Something was left unsaid. Her heart raced at the compassion she heard in his words. Her body sizzled seeing the desire in his eyes. She received that look from men all the time. With Adonis, it felt different; it was different. It was because she loved him.

"You what?" she asked. She had to know.

"I wanted you back then. With everything in me, I did want you back then. When your brother and I were talking after I came back home for a quick visit before heading off for more agent training, he told me about the guy you were going to the prom with. It was the day before the prom. This guy, who had been trying for months to get you to go out with him, chose to not take you to the prom because you were refusing to have sex with him that night. I didn't like that any guy would be pressuring you to do that."

She chuckled remembering what happened the night after the prom. Even though she was angry at Adonis, she appreciated that he stood up for her.

"I bet he has never forgotten the result of the beach party the night after the prom. You beat him up pretty bad. You could have risked your career."

"There was your father, Governor William Mann, saving my ass yet again. I couldn't let him get away with the things I heard he'd been saying about you. He was jealous that I came to the prom with you. He thought he was humiliating you knowing everyone else had already asked girls out to the prom. He thought it would be too late for you since it was the day before when he bowed out."

Gabby shook her head in agreement. Her mind flashed back to the moment her brother told her to get dressed the night of her prom. She was so self-conscious when everyone at school heard what Allistair Washington did to her. She just wanted to graduate and get her music career off the ground. Years of training, acting and singing lessons was about to pay off for her. She had also been picked to sing at their graduation. All eyes would be on her.

Jordan had secured her a limousine. The best part of it all was when the limo pulled up and the side door opened. Out came Adonis in his black tuxedo and tie with accessories that matched her off-white gown. He even had a wrist corsage in his hand along with a dozen long-stemmed red roses. He made sure that she'd had the time of her life. She wanted to return the favor when she asked Victoria for a condom while at the prom because she wanted to go to a hotel with Adonis.

Him turning her down was double the impact on her ego that had taken place when Allistair dropped her as his prom date thinking it was too late for her to get another date. Adonis had been her savior that night. He was still trying to be that.

"You wanted me? Are you saying that now so that I can stop being a diva to you?" she said, smiling lightly.

Adonis reached his hand out to her. Gabby looked at it and then up to his eyes. She was afraid to put her hand in his. She was so weak when it came to him. Going for broke, she did. She allowed him to pull her closer to him. They were no match when it came to height. He was well over six-foot tall and she was a mere five-foot-eight. Great height for a woman, but short when it came to standing close to him. She tried to control her ragged breathing. They hadn't been this close since the prom. She didn't want to count her last night in Miami when he pulled her close to get her quickly in the back of her limo when pandemonium broke out. He was in the shadows but close enough to see what was happening and the fear on her face that caused him to leap into action.

"I know I've been a brute. I can't control that when it comes to you, especially when it pertains to you and Leo. That guy touching or kissing you makes me see fire. I feel like maybe I'm a stalker the way I feel when I see images of the two of you together. I was jealous tonight," he avowed.

"Jealous? Of Leo?" she asked.

Gabby couldn't breathe. Finally, she and Adonis were having a talk from the heart.

"Jealous of you with Leo."

"Why would you be jealous?"

"You're going to make me say it, aren't you?" he jested.

When he laughed slightly, she did also.

"If we're talking and not fighting, I want you to tell me the truth. You've never done that, or at least I thought you had. Now, I feel like I need to question that."

"You should. Like I said, I wanted you. I did back then and I... I... I... do now," Adonis stuttered out.

Gabby didn't know how to take that. What was he admitting to? Loving her? Wanting her could mean so many things. Loving heart would mean everything to her.

"Why did you make jokes about my crush on you? I was serious. Maybe I didn't understand love back then. As I grew older, I knew what I felt back then was true love for you."

"I felt like I would be betraying your family, especially your dad, by getting involved with you."

"I was an adult, not a kid."

"I know. I just didn't see it that way."

"But you did care for me?"

"I did. I cared a lot."

"And you showed it by having sex with women. You and my brother were not shy about the girls y'all brought to the house. I am still amazed at the number of boxes of condoms my brother kept in his room. I assume you had the same. I heard lots of talk about you. I was a woman, but you didn't see me like that. You didn't want me in that way."

"The problem was that I did want you in that way. I couldn't cross that line. I wasn't ready. Truth be told, you weren't ready either."

"I was always ready even when I wasn't. I wanted to show you how much I loved you. I wanted you to know that it wasn't a crush at that age. I was in love with you; I still am," she said.

When she would normally look away from his eyes, she held to them without blinking. It was the middle of the night. All she wanted was for him to want her.

"Gabby."

When Adonis exhaled loudly, she knew that coming clean with her was a struggle for him. She wasn't going to walk away confronting what they were feeling ever again.

"Gabby what?" she came right back with.

She moved even closer to him, locking her fingers with his using both hands. He'd reached for one hand; she just gave him the other. It was now or never and she knew it. For once, they were being completely honest with each other. She needed to know where it was going.

"What are you doing to me?" Adonis asked, shaking his head from side to side as if he was trying to clear it of everything in it.

"Do you truly still want me?" she pleaded.

Adonis moved his head to rest it on her forehead. Gabby raised her hands to either side of his face and held them there. She looked up at his closed eyes and knew that he was letting go of a weight so heavy that she just needed to be here for him. No other time in her life did she ever consider that Adonis was hers. In this moment, he was. He was showing her that he was her all and she was his. She was getting the answer that for years had gone unanswered.

"Yes. Like crazy. I always have. You standing here in my house right now brings it all full-circle. Even though we have had little to no contact all these years, I love you. I think I always have. I've fought it, but dammit, I love you. I know I don't have a right to your love or to even share that I love you. The fight earlier took something out of me. I think I felt what you must have felt when I rejected your love years ago. I meant it when I said I would give my life for you; I would die for you. It's because I love you more than I have ever loved anything or anyone. Knowing that there is someone out there who could hurt you has me losing my mind. I realized what it would mean if Jordan hadn't called me. I shudder to think of what may have happened if I hadn't sent men to your condos to have a look around. Or what may have happened if I wasn't in Miami when your team slipped up. I don't want to think of the person I would become if anything happened to you."

"It didn't. I'm good."

"I've never said these words before. I want to be as open and honest as I can with you. I'm afraid," he admitted.

"Of what?" she asked.

"Of my desire for you."

"What? I don't understand. What are you afraid of?"

"Gabby, if I touch you, I don't know if I'll be able to survive just doing it one time."

"I don't want just one time. Do you still believe that my feelings for you are still an infatuation? What do I need to say or do to get you to believe that wanting you was not a phase in life that I was going to just get over as if you didn't mean everything to me? Your hands on me? Your lips kissing me? Your body loving me? I'm not a child, Adonis."

Gabby leaned forward and kissed his chest through his shirt.

He watched her kiss him once, twice and then a third time before her eyes rose to his. Her beauty is unmatched to any other woman. He closed his eyes and took in the moment.

"Look at me," she said in the same manner that he had done minutes ago.

93

She watched his eyes open slowly, his forehead still resting on hers, his hands now gripping the edge of the counter. He was struggling. One of the toughest, strongest men she knew, a man with the code name, Jaguar, was allowing himself to be vulnerable with her. She didn't take it lightly.

"A.D., and I hardly ever call you that, you are an amazing person. Your confidence is magnetic. Your bravery is admirable. You're always ready to take action. I've seen it a lot growing up in Calabasas. You are fearless. I saw it in Miami. You came out of nowhere and took charge in a dangerous situation. You're not afraid to take risks, even when the odds seem insurmountable, especially when it comes to dealing with me. I know you're risking a lot pouring your heart out to me tonight. You don't know if I will accept or reject it. If I were a bitter woman, I may have chosen the latter. I can't do that. I love you. Nothing is going to happen to me because you're here. I got it. I've been stupid, but not anymore. I will take your lead when it comes to my safety."

"Is that the only place?" he asked, gruffly.

She shivered. Something hot and sexy emitted from his tone. She liked it. She loved it. She wanted to hear it again.

"What else do you have in mind?" she asked.

Gabby didn't know what to expect.

"Indulge me?"

She swallowed hard and loud, preparing for him.

"*Yesssss*," she responded and meant it from the depths of her soul.

She knew that at this point, Adonis could have any request granted; he could have all of her. She was still ready.

In what seemed like one of those slow motion moves in one of her favorite romantic movies, Adonis moved his head down from hers, bringing their lips a whisper away from each other. Her mind screamed with joy. She'd been kissed before, but her ultimate dream man was hopefully about to make a lifelong dream come true. He eyes landed on lips that she wanted to claim her like no other man ever has.

The first soft touch of his lips to hers was amazingly electrifying. A feeling of dizziness took control of her. He kissed her lightly once. Then he repeated that soft touch. Suddenly, Adonis grunted, going back in where he suckled at her lips. He moved desirously from her top lip to her bottom one. He kissed her, by suckling across her lips from one side to the other. Her hands slipped to grip the center of his shirt as his hands came up and cupped her face, holding her mouth to his.

Gabby felt her face flush at the gentle way in which he was handling her. This was Adonis. He wasn't some guy. He wasn't any other guy. He was hers. He was kissing her with a level of craving that had her body screaming for more. She wanted his lips and his hands everywhere. Still, she took the time to savor the moment, moving her lips across his, showing him that she was fully into any and everything with him. Inwardly, she was experiencing the most erotic-filled generated feeling in a kiss that she'd ever had before. She knew that there was something about kissing a man who held her heart that was different than just being kissed for the sake of it.

When he pulled away and closed his eyes again, she felt the loss.

"Gabby? Wait."

She nervously shook her head. They couldn't stop.

"No. Don't stop. Please," she practically begged. "I know what I'm doing. I know what I want."

"Baby, if we go down this road, there is no turning back. That means no Leo or no one else. I don't share, especially not when it comes to you. Are we clear about that?"

"You...you called me baby."

"I always have, just not out loud. Did you hear what I said? I can't go down any road with you that starts with kissing that could lead to more unless it's me and you. Do you get what I'm saying?"

"Yes. A million times, yes!"

Pure lust is what she saw staring back at her. A shiver of unadulterated delight that had been dormant for years came to life with new purpose. Her eyes lowered to Adonis' lips again. Her mind willed for him to join them with hers again. She needed that feeling back if she were going to continue breathing. She couldn't believe that they had kissed. Wow!

Without thinking of the impact, she licked across her own lips. That drew a rasping growl from Adonis. The sound and the look in his eyes spoke of the volume of restraint he'd been holding onto. From the looks of him, he wasn't holding back anymore. His growls turned her on. Between them, she could feel his body hardening in response to this being him and her in this intimate moment. The essence between her legs that she felt moistening the thin strip of her silver thong had her rubbing her legs together.

Adonis parted his lips and landed possessively on her mouth. They were equally panting as they went after each other as if they were starving animals. He loved her mouth with enough electricity to light up the sky. He was asking for an invitation with his tongue to allow it to mate with hers. She offered up a slight moan before offering her response in the form of allowing her own tongue to respond in kind to his.

He deepened the kiss. Her body crackled with fiery love for more. These were new feelings for her. She needed so much more, but only with him. Now was the time.

**

"Where are you?" he asked himself, not speaking to anyone, but yelling at the white brick of Gabby's condo building.

He took a chance that he would spot her going home after seeing her face plastered all over social media. Though it was late, he'd rushed to get dressed to get to the club. His only motivation was to catch a glimpse of her now that she was more easily accessible in the town where he also lived. He had to have her.

When he arrived at the club, luckily, he had the pull to get in even though the crowd was at capacity. When he was first turned away, he asked to speak to the owner or manager. When he was able to share that he could make their lives a living hell, he was escorted inside. He was happy that he knew people.

Knowing Gabby would most likely be in VIP, he headed for that area. His stomach turned to lead when he saw her draped all over Leo. Cameras flashed all about. By now, he could log onto any site and see the photos. They were the hottest couple in town. The idea produced a murderous rage inside of him. He hated everything about seeing the two of them together. He needed to put an end to the game of letter and email writing. The gifts he'd sent to her early on had no impact. It wasn't until he began sending her things that scared her, did she sit up and pay attention. He wondered if his antics in Miami were what sent her into hiding for a week. He was happy to see that she was back to being who he expected Gabby to be; a trick for the media attention.

He smiled knowing that he had planned out every detail of making Gabby his from the moment he'd met her. He only had to make it come to fruition.

Unfortunately, within an hour, he missed when she slipped out of the club. He had hoped she would have gone home. Thinking lady luck was on his side, knowing how to get inside of her condo building, he quickly hopped in his truck and raced to her building. What he didn't think about was the possibility that she'd be spending the night at Leo's place. Before he thought about it, he knew it would be too late to get to his house in the Hollywood hills.

Thoughts of Leo kissing her and doing other things he didn't want to think about made him furious. He was so mad that without thinking, he took out his pocket knife and sliced it into the passenger seat of his own car. The tearing of the leather made him sigh with relief. He was imagining Gabby in the car with him. He was seeing the knife tearing through her. He didn't like a tease. He hated women who didn't see him.

"How dare you let another man touch you? Why were you dressed like a slut tonight anyway? All that you are is for me and me only! Don't you know that? I'll give you one more chance, Gabby. You get one more chance to come to your senses and be mine."

Starting up his truck, he pulled into the light traffic at three in the morning. He would have more chances to make his move. She was back on his turf. She couldn't hide out from him forever. He had a way of finding her. All he needed to do now was get her. If she fought him when he finally got his clutches on her, she would regret it. One way or another, this had to end. He was ready for her.

8

Something Adonis knew and had always feared was that his first touch or first kiss with Gabby would be mind-blowing. He had been right. Now that he had suckled her soft, sweet lips, there was no going back to keeping his distance from her. The way she was responding to him only fueled the storm that was now brewing in his body. His desire for her that had been just on the surface for so long, was now alive, large and in charge. He was hot. His body was scolding with a heated fuse that could only be doused by sinking into her sweetness as far as he could, making them one.

This hadn't been his plan when he came home after hanging out with Cypher. He was ready to let her go back to her place in the morning while he still worked behind the scene. Unprepared for the rush of need for her, he was locked within his love for her. He found himself too far gone. He wanted to love her completely. He wanted to replace the memories she held of feeling like she wasn't enough for him with those that would let her know that she was the only one for him; she always had been and always would be.

A lurid image of them entangled together, writhing together across his bed had him picking her up into his arms and turning toward the steps that led to a bed; his bed. He stopped when he reached the first step. He was experiencing a level of doubt. This was the first time that he'd ever wanted a woman this much. The same issue continued to plague him; this was Gabby.

"You're second-guessing again." she boldly said, before he could even speak.

"You feel so good, so natural in my arms. Your body in my hands, your lips against my lips, your heart beating and feeding the love I carry for you in my own heart; I don't want to mess this up. I want you so damn bad that I ache. If we make love, it will change everything between us," he confessed.

"It will also answer a final question for me. I can't say we should have done this that night, but I do know that we should be doing this now; tonight. You've kissed me. I've tasted you while you've tasted me. I think you know what it means when you said we can't go back. I don't want to. Can you love me now. Please?"

When Gabby initiated the kiss this time, stealing his breath away, Adonis knew he would never again be able to deny her anything; most of all, giving her his love. When her lips left his and pressed softly against the pulse beating rapidly in his throat, he was a goner. The titillating sensations he wished he could fight took over. His legs quickly carried them up the two flights and into his bedroom. The darkened room didn't keep him from seeing all of her as he placed her at the foot of his bed. His eyes caressed over her. His amorous need for her had him confused about what part of her body to love on first.

He sighed when her big, beautiful light brown eyes stared

up at him. With unsteady fingers, he reached for the two straps of her dress that rested on her shoulders. He slid them down her arms before reaching behind her to lower her zipper. An irresistible longing flared hot and unending within him. His fingers lingered on her heated skin. He knew she would be this soft.

"I should have initiated this before now. I've always wanted to," he said against her lips, while his fingers reached for the sides of the dress as he watched it drop to the floor. She stood before him unafraid and not shy in panties he could barely see. Her breasts were like two large delectable melons sitting high on her chest. In his eye, she was extraordinarily beautiful. There isn't a woman who could match her.

Pulling his tank top over his head he tossed the useless piece of clothing out of his way. As much as he wanted to get to her, he wanted her to easily be able to get to him.

"How do you feel?" he asked her.

"Happy. I feel like I wish this moment hadn't taken so long to come."

"I promise to not drag this out. Now is not the time for me to be a tease. I'm afraid the moment I'm inside of you, I'm going to burst out of extreme want way too soon," he said on a slight laugh.

"I will take that knowing that it won't be all that there is; at least I hope not."

"Like I said, there is no going back. Anytime you want me, you only have to look my way. That's all it will take."

When Gabby reached for his gym shorts, he knew she meant business.

"Then be prepared for always; all the time."

"Baby, you prepare."

Slipping her bra and her panties from her body, he took in every inch of her. He moved her to the bed, joining her now that they were both completely naked. Making sure to start their love off right, he pulled a condom from the table beside the bed. Coming back to her, he covered her body with his, whispering her name again and again. His arousal sprang between them, long and thick. His saw Gabby's eyes as they perused all of him.

"I want you so bad," she uttered.

"I have so much I want to do to you; *with* you. You may be used to a lot of foreplay. I am more than into that. I don't want to deny you anything, but I will die a slow death if I don't get inside of you. We'll..."

Gabby stopped him with a smile that grew wider by the second and a finger to his lips.

"Say less; just say less and do more at this point before I combust right here. Together, we'll burst into a ball of flames."

Adonis connected their lips again. He slipped the condom on over his hardness. He was damn sure never in his life had he ever been this hard for a woman before. His length was in pain as it strained in her direction. It was as if his body recognized his need for her and only her.

Adonis spread her legs using his own and lowered his body. With his mouth sharp and feisty against hers, he pulled her close. With a swift move to finally bring them together after making sure her body was ready for his, he reached between her legs. His fingers stroked her womanhood. The amount of warm silky liquid that covered his fingers spoke volumes to how much she was ready for him. He didn't want to make either of them wait. Her hips shimmied around responding to his fingers playing around and inside of her drove him wild.

Positioning himself, Adonis slid slowly into her body until he felt resistance. What he felt was something he had not experienced since he was a teenager. He knew what he was encountering. He stopped moving. His eyes flared wide when he looked at the painful wince on Gabby's face. He picked his words carefully. He had to know.

"Gabby?"

"Don't stop. I know it will only hurt for a little bit and then I'll be okay," she pleaded.

Adonis tried to decipher what was happening. He didn't know how to handle the reality of the moment.

"Wait – you're still…"

Knowing he needed to stop, he pulled out of her body and waited. Exhaling patiently, he reigned in the yearning to surge into her waiting body.

"Yes."

"*How? Why?*"

"What? Should I not be because I'm twenty-six? I'm not an old maid," she lamented.

Immediately, he knew he needed better words.

"Baby, I'm not saying that. You should have told me before we got this far."

"Why? So that you could reject me again?"

"No, dammit. I'm never going to do that again. I promise. I need to know what's happening here. I'm your first?"

When she looked away, as she had a tendency to do when she wanted to avoid his gaze, he turned her head back to him.

"Sad, right?" she asked.

"No, not a sad thing at all. I need to know that this is what you want. You want to lose your virginity with me?"

Gabby nodded.

"I've always wanted to lose it with you. If you must know, I have never allowed a man into my body before. Well, you know that now. That's not to say that I haven't learned how to give my own self powerful orgasms. I didn't want anyone else like that. I only wanted you. It may not have been that way forever, but it was certainly what it's been up until now. Does that mean you don't want to make love with me? I know how men of a certain age can be about virgins."

"Baby, you're not just any virgin. You're a woman I love. I'm honored to be the first man to love you like this. It's not a bad thing. I wish I had known before we started."

"Are we done?"

Adonis winked at her. He wanted to take any tension out of the moment.

"Not by any means. I'm going to slow things down. I want to be sure you're enjoying every minute of your first time. It doesn't change that I love you and I want you."

When Gabby nodded, he leaned forward and kissed her back into their loving moment. Instead of attempting to enter her body again, he slid down her curves, kissing her along the way. Her moans of pleasure encouraged him on. Next, he parted her legs and kissed her intimately along the thin strip of hair that led to the center of her womanhood. The minute her hips leapt from the mattress, his new approach was where they needed to be. They would talk later. This moment was meant for love; a love that was a long time coming.

With his lips and tongue, he loved her slowly. His hands reached up her body to caress her breasts. She easily creamed in his mouth. Gabby's moans grew louder. Her hips thrashed about.

He found the nub that needed all of his attention. Centering on it, he sucked it, letting his tongue smooth over it again and again. He slid a single finger into her body, moving it in an out slowly before picking up the speed. In a move that had Gabby calling his name again and again, he added a second finger inside of her. By the time her orgasm had her screaming with delightful cries he knew that together, they were focused on how her body reacted to him. He never wanted to forget the moment that the woman he loved admitted that she'd saved her body for him and only him. If he didn't know that they were joined for life before now, this moment sealed that for him. He hoped she was ready for forever with him. He said no turning back and he meant it.

With his fingers still inside of her, milking every drop he could from her body, moved quickly to cover her body, kissing her deeply.

"You taste like honeysuckle deliciousness. I love every drop that's covering my face. I'm going to love, loving you," he said against her lips.

"That was amazing," Gabby slurred out, still in a haze from her release.

"I wanted to do a better job of preparing you for what's next. It will be a little painful, but I promise, it will also get a lot better. Are you ready for me to try again?"

Gabby nodded.

Taking great care this time while realizing as he gripped himself that he was actually even harder than he was on his first attempt at entering her body. He needed to go slow. Nine inches for a virgin would hurt like hell, but women, he knew were resilient. One day, he was already imaging that Gabby would be bearing his children. He would be by her side for that pain as well.

"I'm ready," she stuttered out.

"If I hurt you, tell me to stop or slow down. We got all the time in the world. As much as I've waited for this, this is about you and your pleasure. Hold onto me, baby," he whispered against her cheek.

With care, Adonis slid back into her body. This time, her orgasm had paved the way with enough slickness to ease some of the pain he knew was coming her way. Moving his hips slowly, he gave her more of him and watched for her reaction. She felt so good and definitely tight, but he would control his desire to drive further into her. This was the woman he loved. It wasn't about the act; it was about the love.

Adonis watched emotion flare across Gabby's face. Instinctively, he pulled out and slowly gave her more of him. When he finally crossed the barrier and she flinched, he lay still above her. He had to give her time to adjust.

"Baby?" he crooned into her neck, kissing her there. He could feel her hands gliding up and down his arms.

"I'm okay. I promise I am."

He did love her then. His hips moved with purpose. He gathered her into his arms. They moved together. The pace he'd set was a slow one. It was Gabby who was first to increase the speed of their loving. He followed her lead. Within moments, he was loving her hard and deep. Her body responded to him like a woman who'd been loved before, but he knew she hadn't been. He was on the brink of losing control as they climbed higher and higher.

"Yes, Adonis!" she screamed. Gabby's hips met his stroke for stroke.

A sexy whimper escaped her lips. Adonis pumped into to

her. She stuttered unintelligible words. He needed to feel her let go for him before he did. He was close. He could tell by the way her breathing hitched and increased that she was close. Reaching between them, he stroked her. He nipped on her neck. They were ready for endless pleasure.

"Yes, yes, yes!" she screamed.

Gabby's hips bucked wildly. She held to his shoulders, her nails digging in slightly. Bracing his hands on either side of her, he used only his hips to prolong her enjoyment. Within seconds, his toes curled and his own body took a flying leap off the ledge and into a sexual bliss. His screams were as loud as Gabby's were as they rode out their mutual pleasure together.

When Gabby drew in a deep breath and collapsed under him, Adonis slowed his hips, but kept moving. He felt her body quiver through lasting quakes that wouldn't let her go. This is the kind of enjoyment he wanted to be sure she had. Looking down into her eyes, he could see that he had given her, not just her first orgasm by way of intercourse, but he'd given her his brand of unconditional and unwavering love.

"Did I hurt you?" he asked.

"No. That was amazing. Oh, my goodness, that was nothing like giving myself an orgasm with a toy. I hope that's not too much information," she giggled.

When she leaned up to find his lips, Adonis made it easy for her by closing the gap between their faces.

"For me, hell no. I'm going to put that on the back burner as a reserve to be sure I get to see you in action for myself. I think it's hot."

"Will I get to see you?" she asked.

"What? Pleasure myself?"

"Yes."

"Baby, after what we just shared, I would give you anything. If you have a pen, I'll write out the passcode to my bank account. You are amazing. You're also mine."

His mouth found hers as her hands wiped, what he knew, was a large amount of sweat from his brow.

"No one else, Adonis. Never, ever."

"This is love," he said.

9

Adonis came fully away expecting to reach for Gabby. To his dismay, the other side of the bed was empty. The bright sun of a new day greeted him when he opened his eyes. Though he felt around for her, he had to see with his own eyes that she wasn't there. After having her in his arms all night, he wanted the same for the morning. Inhaling, he did notice the smell of turkey bacon wafting across his nose. She was cooking.

Listening closely, he could hear her singing in the kitchen. Her angelic voice drew him in. He heard how she easily wooed her fans. He lay flat on his back with his hands behind his head to enjoy the moment of her sweet voice fanning across the house. Grabbing for his phone, he was shocked at the number of calls he missed. Most shocking was the late hour of the morning. He very seldom slept late. I had to be the loving from a good woman that had knocked him out cold.

He and Gabby had made love a second time after which he drew her a hot bath. He didn't want her body to be sore from their lovemaking two times in one night that was her first time. While she sat in the tub, he had pulled together a bowl of fruit and a little of the shrimp salad that she'd already taken out. After putting the rest away for them to enjoy later, he walked into the bathroom to check on her and found her asleep. He easily lifted her from the tub, wrapping her in a large, thick blue towel. She woke as he was drying her body. His heart thumped loudly in his chest when even while half-asleep, Gabby whispered over and over how much she loved him. She never stopped as he took his time drying every part of her body. When he placed her in bed and crawled in next to her, her arms reached out for him while her words continued to call out to him. He pulled her close, spooning her body to his. The last thing he remembered was whispering over and over to her how much he loved her and that he always wood. Feeling like he could rest forever just like that, he had joined her in peaceful sleep.

In the light of day, all that they had shared brought a smile to his face. He still needed answers from her which he planned on getting before they made love again. There was no doubt that after the way they connected, pretty much perfectly in bed, that they would be indulging again before the sun went down. His body drummed with a desire to love her now. First up, the talk.

Rising, he slipped on his gym shorts from the evening before and headed toward the kitchen. Gabby was in his house and he needed a morning kiss.

When he reached the bottom step, he stopped and watched her. Soft music was playing. His eyes landed on her hips swaying sexily to the beat.

"Good morning, beautiful," he said walking up behind her, his hands on her hips. After pressing his lips longingly on the back of her neck, he groaned into it when the grinding of her hips was directed at that part of him that was already hard for her.

Gabby turned around and before he could provide the invitation to a morning kiss, she took what she wanted and needed from his lips. He more than obliged her.

"Good morning to you, sleepyhead. I thought you would never get up. I've been up for over an hour."

He swatted her soft behind and laughed when she playfully shrieked.

"I see that you've been busy. You've opened all of the blinds and started breakfast. I smelled bacon and it pulled me out of bed."

"We don't just have bacon. I found turkey sausage in your fridge, waffle mix in the pantry and the waffle maker. How is it that you have all of these things in a house you are barely ever in?"

"When I do come home from a mission, I lock myself in here for days. I like to relax and work on myself. It sometimes takes me a minute to join the world where I don't have a weapon in my hands. I enjoy having what I like at my fingertips. Speaking of..."

Adonis' words trailed off. He reached again for Gabby, pulling her to him with his fingertips. This time when they kissed, he held her lips to his, coaxing her mouth open for a much deeper and more satisfying joining.

"Bacon burning," Gabby said before moving out of his reach to check the air-fryer.

"How do you feel?" he asked.

When she looked over her shoulder at him, awareness of why he was asking covered her face.

"A little sore, but I'm sure it would have been worse if not for the bath you drew for me. Sorry I fell asleep in the middle of it. It was so soothing. I felt like I was in a deep sleep."

"Did you sleep okay in bed with me?"

"I slept perfectly. Will I be sleeping there tonight?" she asked.

"What did I say about that, Gabby?"

"This is us. We're not going backward and you're mine!" she yelled and laughed.

"And?"

"I'm yours," she added.

"Exactly. If you're here, there is no more guestroom for you. I'm going to have the housekeeper take care of resetting the bedding for guests in that room where you've been camped out. She'll be here tomorrow for her usual day of cleaning."

"I have a rehearsal tomorrow. Can you ask her to move my things upstairs or am I being too presumptuous that she would do things for me? When I'm home, I use a service. It's not often the same person."

"Consider it on my list. She'll take care of it. Can I get Ray to drive you to your rehearsal?"

"The big guy from Miami?"

He was glad Gabby remembered him.

"Sure. What about my people?"

"I don't want to cut anyone out of a job. I plan to meet with your agent to discuss security. You good with that?" he asked.

"I trust you."

Adonis nodded knowing that a lot had already changed just since last night. He was expecting pushback from her, but instead, her admission that she knew all his effort was to

113

protect her was resonating in the light of day.

Walking around the island, he pushed the button on the Keurig to brew a cup of coffee. For several minutes, they moved about the kitchen doing different things. Gabby mixed up the batter for waffles while he made a list of things that he wanted his housekeeper to pick up. She already knew what to do around the house.

Unlike Gabby, he used the same woman to help out around his house. He didn't want a bunch of different people in and out especially when he wasn't around. He trusty Myra. She was a mother figure in his life who took great care of him. He was sure to get a strange look from her once he makes the request to have Gabby's things moved to his room. In the years that Myra has been his housekeeper, she has never known for him to move a woman's things into his bedroom. It was rare that one actually spent the night. He preferred waking up in his bed alone. That is until Gabby. Now, he can't image not having her there.

Having Gabby in his home was a good idea. He wondered what it would take to keep her here. He didn't want to put pressure on her or interfere in the life she should be able to live as a woman making her own decisions. He would love to have her close, but also knew that she would one day have to go back home to her own place. The work on her condo was being completed by the end of day. There would be no reason for her to stay with him.

After the silence in the room drove him crazy, he brought up a subject he knew she didn't want to talk about. He'd tried a few times after they made the first time. To distract him, Gabby had grabbed another condom and asked him to show her how to please him by her being on top. He'd done just that. She had rocked his world off of its foundation. She left him dog-tired and in an exhaustive state after a powerful orgasm. When he attempted to think clearly with no blood left in his head or his feet, to his own ears, he sounded like a bumbling idiot. If it was her plan to keep him from bringing up the fact that she was a virgin, it had worked. He forgot about it until now.

"Gabby, can we talk this morning. No distracting me with sex either. I peeped your game last night. It worked and you were good. I'm thinking a repeat if your body isn't too tender to do so."

She didn't stop moving about the kitchen. He was already discovering and picking up on her little quirky ways. It was as cute as she was gorgeous.

"This body is already craving you. One night and I want a lot more. I had no idea sex was that amazing. I wish I had indulged years ago."

"Not me."

"I'm still talking about only with you."

He was happy when Gabby cleared that statement up. He no longer had to think of another man making love to her.

Adonis chuckled at her jubilance around the topic.

"That's what I want to talk about. Can you stop moving long enough for us to talk?"

He saw her shoulders slump. She was relenting because there was no escape. He could clearly see that she wasn't wearing panties or a bra. There would be no storming out of the house on him this time when he wanted to bring up a topic that she would rather avoid.

"Why?"

"Why, what?"

"Why do we need to talk about it. You know now. What else is there?"

"Baby, I don't want you to be uncomfortable when it comes to talking to me. Talking to me is a safe space. It always will be for you. You have to admit that I should be curious, and I am. I've thought back over the years and you've been linked to a few good men and some not so good, like Leo. Leo! Let's start there. That brother is known for his sexual prowess. How the hell have you been together this long with no sex? What's going on there? Is your relationship with him strictly for publicity's sake?" he asked.

"Yes. My label put us together thinking we could boost each other's careers. It worked. We are both at the top of the charts. Venues pay us to show up as a couple knowing our fans will show up to see us. We attend red carpet events as a couple because we look good together. We put on a show for the cameras. It's all Hollywood," she suggested.

"Does anyone outside of your label who hasn't signed a non-disclosure agreement know?"

"Yes. Victoria, Sierra and my family. Leo is too much of a manly-man to let anyone think that he would be drawn into a fake relationship for image and ratings sake."

"Guys you've been linked to before that? What about them?"

"You've been gone for a while. There haven't been that many. I don't sleep around, as you now know. I don't allow any story written about me to put that out in the atmosphere."

"Has Leo tried?"

Adonis didn't know if he was ready for the answer. He thought back to his reaction to her high school prom date. He was remembering the rage he took out on him. Leo wouldn't stand a chance against him either.

"What are you going to do?"

"About what?" he asked.

"If I say, yes."

"I'm not going to do anything. I'm not that twenty-three-year-old guy anymore. I'm thirty-one and I know better. That's not the answer. Also, last night before we made love, I was jealous of him. Knowing what I do know now, there is nothing to be jealous of. He's not a factor. I just want to know."

"Yes, he tried a lot; even last night. He kept asking me to go back to his place from the club. I reminded him I was out because I'm under contract, not for pleasure. I assume he did what he always does."

"What's that?"

"Have his team sneak in a bunch of women who would sign NDAs for a night of fun with him. I understand he pays very well for the silence of other women as not to harm his career if the truth got out."

"And now? If he touches you, I'm going to break every bone in both of his hands."

Whether he was joking or serious, he didn't know. When Gabby looked at him, it was clear that she wasn't sure of his seriousness either.

"You can't do that. I told you it's nothing. Any kind of touch is purely platonic and for us to be camera-ready."

"Ever kiss him for the cameras? I mean on the lips, not just one of those friendly for the camera-type kisses."

"Adonis? What's going on?"

"I'm jealous, humor me. Well?"

"No, I have never locked lips with him or any man in the past year or so. I have actually dated before Leo. I've just abstained from sex. Being that kind of woman, long-lasting relationships were not on the horizon for me. We live in a day and time where sex is supposed to be a given simply because you meet someone. I have always wanted it with someone I was in love with; hence, last night. I would have done it with you back on prom night if you had wanted to. I want you to know that I would have."

"The fact that you placed a condom in my palm while we were dancing that night was a pretty big sign."

"It was, right? I had to eventually tell Victoria a lie that we'd had sex and how good it was. Now I can actually speak that from experience. Thanks for being patient with me last night. I know a man of your prowess didn't find that easy."

"While I may not be a virgin, I also do not bed every woman I cross or who comes for me. I'm more selective."

"Have you been in a relationship with any woman? Since we're playing twenty questions, I'd like to add some too."

"My job has interfered with that for most of my adult life. I was recruited pretty much after my senior year in high school. My college was paid for, a burden I didn't want to fall on your father or Mr. Basheer anymore. Those two men changed my life. I was focused on my career. That's why I wasn't home often between eighteen and twenty-two. It was intense and took up most of my life. Then I went into the field and I wasn't in any one place long enough for anything long term."

"And now?"

"I love you. I don't want anyone else but you," he confirmed.

Gabby put batter on the waffle maker and then walked over to him. He made room for her when she slid between his legs as he sat on the stool at the counter. Taking his coffee cup from his hands, she put it down and put his hands on her ass cheeks. They equally smiled after hearing the loud slapping sound. He would bank the idea of doing that again later.

"What you are feeling right now, Mr. Duquette, is part of what is all yours. You put your claim on all of me last night. It's how I've always wanted it to be and it's how it will always be. You said you would give up your life for me, right? You have to know that the way that I have always loved you, I would do the same thing. That's more fact than you'll ever get from anyone. You may not know this, but I know what your high security clearance means. I know that your life could be in jeopardy if your real identity was compromised while you're under on a case. Jordan once sat us all down and made us aware of how much danger we could put you in if we didn't take great care in who we know you are."

"Yeah, he and I had a lot of conversations about my life as an agent."

"He told us that. He once said, if any of us were out in public and we saw you, unless you came directly up to us to greet us, we were to act as if we didn't know you. He said if he was not on a case, he would always approach us first. If he was on one, he would act as if he never knew us from Adam and Eve. I know what that means. Jordan was very clear and specific about our interactions with you. I love you, A.D.

Duquette. I have no problem doing red carpets, clubs, concerts, etc., without a man on my arm. If you say you don't like the façade I have to put on with Leo, I understand. You need to believe me when I say there is nothing there. I'm in this with you from this point forward until the wheels fall off. I'm assuming that's going to be never," Gabby explained.

"Yes, that's pretty much never. I understand your life. Thanks for understanding mine. We are some pair, huh?"

Racing to check on the waffle, Gabby nodded her affirmation.

"Do you want butter or margarine on your waffle? You have both; I checked."

He chuckled at how domesticated they were already being. He never saw this for him. Already, he never wanted to be in this life without it.

"A small dab of both. What can I do to help? You know I love to cook?"

"Nothing. I was hoping you could think of something good to cook us later like your spaghetti and fresh garlic bread. I've got breakfast. This is my last day of relaxation. I need to get ready for my upcoming shows. Oh, I forgot that later today, I need to meet with the choreographer. I want to bring in an all-girl group of dancers for my final show. I need her to get on top of working with them. There isn't a lot of time to prepare."

"I'll be at your condo for a few hours today. I want to look over the work that was done. I'll be done in time to whip us up a nice meal for later. How much time do you have before you leave?"

"Just enough time. Make the time count!" she quipped.

"I got you."

Checking their food again, Gabby turned toward him with tongs in her hands pointing them at him.

"Guess who I saw last night?" she asked.

He hunched his shoulders. He had no clue.

"I'm all ears, baby."

"Brien. I don't know if you've met him before."

"I don't think so, but I have heard Jordan mention him a lot. Why did it stand out that you saw him?"

"He was acting all weird as if he didn't want me to see him."

"You saw Brien, where?"

"At the club. I wouldn't think that the club scene was a place he would ever be caught alive in. He even looked out of place. He caught my attention really fast. I was in VIP with my team and Leo's team and I looked over to see him at the bar. He wasn't dancing or drinking or anything. I started to go down to say hello but then I got caught up when I was asked to sing a song. I looked his way and when he looked my way at the same time, it was as if he didn't want me to see him. he jerked body around and purposely hid himself behind a group of men near the bar. It was odd. After I sang, I slipped out the back and had Leo's driver bring me back here."

Adonis' radar went up. He didn't think it meant anything, but the special ops man he was, everyone was suspect. He said the threat had to be someone close. What if it was someone not close to her but close to someone else who was close to her? He made a mental note to have everyone in her family's circle checked out too.

"Have you ever seen him at any of your other shows?" he questioned.

He waited knowing she was thinking about it.

"Now that you mention it, I think I saw him at my show in Miami and at the Chicago show. That would be ridiculous right? I mean, he works for my brother and he's busy here in Los Angeles. It couldn't have been him. Looked like him though. Anyway, there is a guy I was dating a while back who turned into quite the stalker when I broke things off. Again, sex came into play and I said no. He was another man who taught me that until I was ready for that next step, I need not try and really date. Having Leo as a stand-in takes the pressure off. I was able to really focus on getting my career where it is now. Did I tell you how much I love being here with you? I haven't had this much peace in my life – not in years. I was always on the go attending something that kept me moving. I would find myself about to relax before deciding that wasn't for me and I'd hit up an event in order to be seen. Here, there is paparazzi. They would be outside of my condo. I would come out of the label offices and cameras would be shoved in my face. I went to the premiere of the latest Fast and Furious movie and it was crazy. I wore this red Vera Wang gown, hair down my back and you know, being cute and all. When the attention should have been on the stars, it was on me. Sometimes, I admit, I don't realize how popular I am. Being here in this house, I don't care anything about that. I know I gave you grief about feeling like a prisoner here, but that was a bold-faced lie. You've helped me realize that condos are nice, but a house on the beach with no public access is perfection. If I lived like this all the time, I would be able to enjoy the tranquility that I sometimes long for. You've provided this space for me. Leo once offered me a wing of his house. That would have been a terrible idea for more reasons than just a few. He's just as well-known as I am. That wouldn't have worked like it works with me being here."

"That's because no one knows about me. They won't be able to find you here. Remember to always enter and exit a car in the garage. You didn't do that last night. I'll have to remember to leave one side of the garage open for a car to drive you in, lower the garage door and then open it to back out once you're in the house."

"Do you really think the threat is still there? I've been here over a week and there hasn't been any letters, emails, pictures, nasty gifts or anything. Maybe he's found a new focus, whoever he is."

"Maybe so."

Adonis' years as an agent told him that the threat wasn't gone. It could be that since she's been out of the spotlight and off of people's radar while being at his house, her stalker could simply be regrouping to reappear when she's back out in public.

"Breakfast is ready. I know you don't like a lot of eggs. Did you want me to scramble you some?" she asked.

"No, I have all I need. In fact, come here," he said, winking lustfully at her.

Without hesitating, Gabby came back to her place between his legs. When the top she was wearing rose up, he looked down and behind her to get a glimpse of her backside. He was having ideas about a view from the back just like that when he made love to her again.

When she kissed him, Adonis' brain turned to mush. Her body in his hands was all he needed to know that he was no longer hungry for breakfast.

"You're a mind reader now?" he questioned against her lips, now moistened just for him.

"I take it we're not about to eat breakfast?" she asked when he stood and like last night, picked her up in his arms.

"Any burners on?" he questioned with sexy activities on his brain.

"No. We can heat up the food later."

"Good to know. I have a different kind of feast I'd like to partake in since my time with you is limited today. Are you coming back here tonight? Your condo will be upgraded and ready for you?"

He hoped to hear her say no. It was her choice. He would follow her lead.

"I don't care. I'm coming back here to be with you. You're making dinner, remember?"

"Right. I got that covered. I'm going to take a trip down to the local FBI office to ask a few questions. I still want Ray to pick you up here at the house and make sure you get back. We good?"

Gabby nodded and winked.

"We're perfect. Anything else before I forget there isn't a condom down here. You're poking me and it would be really easy access with me not having any panties on," she quirked.

"Mmm, you planned it that way. I'm a starving man, but not for food."

"Love me again?"

"You're sure? You have rehearsal. You don't want to be walking and dancing around grimacing from soreness. This is new for you," he said marching them hurriedly to the stairs.

"I have Tylenol. We'll leave time for another soak in the tub. I don't want you to take it easy on me. I want it all; all of you – hard, long and as deep as you can get."

"I aim to please," he said taking the steps two at a time.

"Yes, you do!" Gabby said, pumping her fist in the air as he raced.

10

Victoria waited patiently for Gabby to answer the phone. She had tried her minutes earlier for a video chat meeting and didn't get a response. Calling her number for the third time, she expected to get her voicemail again. To her luck, Gabby answered sounding as if she'd been in a deep sleep.

"Gabby, are you really sleeping in the middle of the day? What is going on with you?"

Victoria spent a lifetime of being Gabby's best friend. This is the first time that she could ever recall Gabby sleeping this late. She'd been missing in action for a few weeks. Her absence has been noted all over social media. She wasn't as concerned as some of Gabby's fans. Even her team at the record label wasn't concerned. She had just gotten off of a three-hour meeting with them. The fact that Gabby wasn't on the call shocked everyone.

Earlier in the morning, Gabby left her a voicemail message asking that, as her assistant, she let the team know that they should come through her with any needs or updates. Gabby decided that she needed a full day to herself. Victoria knew that Gabby had been doing that a lot in the month since her return to Los Angeles. She was happy to see her slow down. Gabby had been running on all cylinders for almost a year.

"What?"

She could hear Gabby moving around. She even heard a slight groan.

"Am I disturbing you? You sound tired. What in the world have you been doing?"

She could almost see her best friend grinning through the phone.

"You don't want to know; or maybe you do," Gabby said happily.

"Sis, tell me, are you still at Adonis' place? You haven't moved back to your place yet? Didn't he give it the all clear a few weeks ago?"

"You are full of a lot of questions this early in the morning," Gabby huffed.

"Early in the morning? Do you know what time it is there? Gabby, it's two in the afternoon."

"Two? Really? If that's the case, I just had the best nap of my *life*.

Yes, I am still at Adonis' place. We are enjoying being under one roof. He's relaxed as he had planned to do while he has time off. I'm more relaxed than I have been in years. That's saying something. I'm usually flying around the country being the life of the party. I had no idea I was missing out on the perfect life."

"Wait? Are you not happy in your career anymore? I just spent the better part of three hours getting instructions from the label about their plan for you. Luckily, they weren't upset that you couldn't make the meeting knowing what you went through in Miami. They are hoping you're ready to hit the road for some promotional touring after your tour ends."

"Absolutely not."

Victoria paused. That wasn't the response she had expected.

"Did you say no? I didn't think you knew that word. You're Gabby Mann. You say yes to everything when it comes to your career."

"That's how things were. They're not like that anymore."

"My goodness. What did Adonis *do* to you? He's got you that whipped? I get it that you've been waiting for this man a long time. Sounds like it's been worth it. Are you giving up on your career to be with him?"

"Again, absolutely not. I'm *investing* in me; in all of me. That includes much more than my career. Right now, that means investing in what I'm building with Adonis. I love my career. I love singing and performing and I intend to do that. I've been doing a lot of writing. You should hear the songs. I have. Adonis moved the piano from my condo to his place. I've been playing and writing like a possessed woman. I want to record. I've seen all of the requests from artists who are interested in working with me. I have been reading all of your emails."

"The list is growing weekly, Gabby. You've been quiet so I haven't pushed. The songs you wrote for yourself that have topped the charts for months have garnered an interest in partnerships with some of the biggest artists in the business."

"What does the label have on their agenda?"

Victoria opened up her iPad to go over the long list of notes she took from the meeting.

"Top on their list is the promotional tour. They've agreed that you could use some time to regroup. I think they were hoping that the time you've taken before these last few concert dates coming up next week would be enough. I'm assuming that's not true."

"You are assuming correctly. Do you realize that I have been on the go for the past three years non-stop? I didn't understand the value of being still. Adonis has this lounge chair, which I'm currently relaxing on. It faces the ocean. When I'm laying down with the chair facing the large window, all I see is water. It's the most beautiful and serene view that anyone could ever experience. I've never taken the time to enjoy the view of the ocean. I love laying here watching it and just dreaming. I can clear my head. I can focus. I can reflect on what I thought was most important to me. I've spent more time with my brother in the past month than I have in years. My parents are coming to town in a few weeks. We're planning a big family trip to Australia. Even Jordan is going to take some time off to come with us."

"Does he know?" Victoria asked, hesitantly.

"Does he know what?"

"Does he know that you and Adonis are playing in the sheets? I assume he must know something since you're still at his place and you could be at home."

"I don't know. He has asked and I haven't offered. Adonis asked me about that. He wants to have a sit down with Jordan since they're best friends. I don't think it's necessary. He probably suspects. We do keep things lowkey when he's here. Besides, I've been busy with my writing and Adonis has been spending time at the auto customizing businesses he owns with his friend Trent."

"Do you think Jordan will be okay with it?"

"I'm sure he will. I want time to have Adonis to myself

before roping my family into my relationship with him."

"So, that's it? You're officially in a relationship? This is new for you."

"I am and yes, it is. It's amazing. He's amazing. We are incredible together."

"I still can't believe you lied to me all these years. You let me walk through life thinking you and Adonis did the deed back then. I was angry at him thinking he left you afterward; breaking things off. The worst part is you let me believe that."

Victoria was serious but also gracious at the same time. She understood why Gabby kept her secret.

"I know. I've apologized profusely. I'm even going to take you out for a girl's day of shopping and pampering, all on me, when you get here. You're still coming for a visit? I also want to say something else to you without being too intrusive in your decision-making."

"Speak away. I'm listening," Victoria said.

Being home alone in her New York City apartment, Victoria rose from her home office and moved quickly to her favorite couch, placing her laptop on her lap. Gabby sounded like she was about to go deep. She needed to be comfortable for that.

"I really want you to consider the offer from the label – more now than ever."

"Gabby? Why is this so important for you? I've been your assistant for a lot of years. I mean, ever since you started your career. Is there an issue with the work I'm doing?" she asked.

"No. Not at all. You know better than to even ask me that. I couldn't have gotten this far without you. Trust is important to me. It's critical in any personal and business relationship. I trust you with both. I knew the new position was opening. You would be working directly for the label president. It's no easy task getting anyone into that seat. I rave about you all of the time. They know the great job you've done for me. Most times, they reach to you before they even think about reaching directly to me. That's how much they trust you as I do."

"I appreciate the confidence you've always had in me."

"Vicki, there is so much more you can learn. You'll have the chance to grow beyond where, working directly for me and only me, can get you. That's what I want for you. Besides, I mean it when I say that I'm taking stock in my life, especially my career. I don't want my life's decisions to impact your life. Think about how much you would love living out here. Admit that every time you come to L.A., it's hard for you to leave. I know you stay in New York for family purposes in order to help your sister with her kids. Her husband passing away was sudden. You stepping in to help her with the kids was a big move for you. I don't want to take you away from that. What if your sister says she doesn't want you to hold back any part of your life for her and the kids? I think it's time you think about it. Just think through the possibilities and let me know."

Victoria thought about her sister, Melissa. Her brother-in-law, Jacob, was diagnosed with an inoperable tumor on his brain. Melissa had just given birth to their third child, her nephew Zion. Just before his second birthday, Jacob got really sick. A month later, he was gone. Melissa fell into a depression. With three small children under the age of six, that was a lot. Moving to New York to help keep some semblance of normalcy in the life of the kids is why she up and changed her entire life around. She was grateful that Gabby never missed a beat in keeping her in her current position. They had the greatest of friendships. Neither of them ever gave each other bad advice. The love of sisters from another mister was strong between them.

"I can't wait to come visit. Melissa is taking the kids to spend two weeks with my parents. They are living the life since moving to the Outer Banks in North Carolina. The timing is perfect for me to visit you. I know we've talked about the job before. You don't have to say much more. I've talked with Melissa about moving to L.A. She's practically packing my bags already. She told me that I've given up enough of my life to help her and the kids. She appreciates it. Foremost, she wants to see me live life for me. After my breakup from Anthony, I could use a new view each morning."

When Gabby shrieked on the other end, she knew it was a sound of happiness.

"See? That's what I'm talking about. Besides, with Anthony being history in our lives, and yes, I said ours, I have someone I want you to meet. Adonis has this friend named Raymond who is perfect for you. Let Adonis introduce you. I'm telling you, this guy is the one for you. I've gotten to know him over the past few weeks. I can see the two of you together. Not only that, he's fine girl!"

"Gabby! Stop it. Do not try and set me up with anyone. What if I come out there and I end up preferring to be in New York?"

"That's crazy talk. No one comes to this coast and then decides that New York is better. That's never going to happen. I won't push. Think about it. You're coming out for two weeks, right?"

"Yes. Two whole weeks. I can't wait to see you. I'm going to be front and center for your final night of your tour. It's going to be exciting and electric."

"I'm looking forward to it for more than it being my last hoorah before taking a break. It's the break that has me on cloud nine. To keep from burning out, the break I'm thinking about is longer than what the label is imagining. I know we're supposed to talk about all of the work they talked to you about this morning to relay to me. I'm only obligating myself to what is already under contract. I'm not signing any new contracts. I want to relax here, in the ocean on the private beach and most of all, in bed with Adonis. The things that man does to me should be illegal. I'm having an enjoyable time being a woman without being a star. That's all I want."

"I hear that. You deserve it. Most of all, you deserve to be this happy and with Adonis. I still remember the day you showed up at the prom on his arm. I think all the high school girls were jealous, including me. There was so much talk after, you know who, backed out. Then you stroll in with the hottest, hunkiest man alive. To know that you waited for him speaks to how you were always meant to be a couple in love."

"You and Ray could have that too, if you let Adonis set you up."

"If he's all that, why isn't he taken?"

"Because he's waiting for you," Gabby asserted.

"You already told him about me? Tell me you didn't do that. I would sound all desperate for a man if I have to be set up," Victoria lamented.

"Don't worry. I haven't said a word to him. I wouldn't let you look like that. He's recently divorced. He's not seeing anyone seriously at the moment. Look at all that could be waiting for you here besides me."

"I do love that city. I grew up there. And the job does sound good. What about being your assistant? I love working with you daily."

"You'll be at the label. We will still work together. I want a lot for you as my sister-girl. This is the road for you. I won't even speak on the money you'll be making."

"I make a lot with you."

"And you still will. That's not going to change. I'm grateful for you. Think of this as two big salaries. I'm going to pick you up when you arrive."

"By yourself?"

"Yes. I've done that a million times before."

"I know. Things are so crazy. I didn't think you would want to be trudging around by yourself."

"I'm good. I keep telling Adonis and the label that I want a little space between me and the hovering crew. It'll be fine. I'll be in disguise. Plus, you're arriving at night. People haven't seen me in so long, I bet they've forgotten what I look like. The braids are out. The weave is out. What you'll see is all me. Most people don't know me if I'm not glammed up," Gabby joked.

"You will never be unrecognizable. You'll be back at your place this week then?"

Victoria assumed, as with always, during her visit, she would be staying with Gabby at her place."

"If not, you'll have my whole condo to yourself. The place is locked down tight. Adonis is sure of that. You can also stay here with us. He has the guest room. It's always ready for guests."

"Hmm, that's because he no longer has a guest in it. You moving into his bedroom is a sure sign that you're not planning to go back to your condo. I get it. As your best friend, I approve."

"He put it on me just that good!" Gabby cheered.

"Who put it on you?"

Victoria heard Adonis' voice in the background.

"Uh oh. Sounds like we've been caught. Do you want to connect this evening to go over everything?" Victoria asked.

"Let's do that. I have a man who just picked me up and sat me on his lap. He looks a little thirsty; hungry even," Gabby laughed.

Victoria could hear loud kissing sounds.

"At least let me hang up before you start! Dang!"

When she heard Gabby giggling, Victoria hung up before her ears encountered too much.

She moved her laptop from her lap and stood. Walking over to look out over Central Park, she smiled at the idea that she could really thrive if she took a leap of faith and made a move to the west coast. Her sister has been encouraging her for months. Perhaps, it was time.

**

"So, I put it on you? I do hope that was me you were talking about?" Adonis questioned.

"Of course, I was talking about you. There is no other man I would ever speak that way about. I thought you were working out? When I came down here to catch a nap in front of this perfect view, you were lifting weights."

Gabby snuggled into Adonis more with her legs on the outside of his.

"I was in the mood for a different kind of workout. Was that Victoria you were talking to?"

"It was. Remember I told you she was coming for a visit this week?"

"Right. You going home while she's here?"

"I thought about it and the answer is no. She'll love having my whole place to herself. I love being here. You ready for me to leave? Have you tired of me already?" she teased.

Adonis grabbed her behind and moved his hands all across her cheeks.

"No panties? I love you with no panties. Talk about easy access."

Gabby kissed his waiting lips.

"Thank goodness for birth control. We don't have to run upstairs for a condom. All you would need to do is slide your shorts down," she started explaining while doing just that with her hands.

When he lifted to make it even easier, Gabby moaned her pleasure against his face.

"With your legs already open for me with two perfect views in front of me, I wouldn't deny you anything. Your beauty and the ocean behind you, just perfection at its best," he slurred against her neck.

Adonis looked down to where Gabby gripped his penis in her hand, at least as much of him as she could get her hands around. When she rose with her head falling backward, his pulse quickened. Gabby centered her body over him. He thought she would be soft and gentle, but instead, she moved down on him hard, causing them both exhale with delight.

"Damn!" Gabby screamed.

Letting her have the control she wanted, Adonis held onto her behind and pumped up into her body fiercely rough and driving into her deeply.

"Baby!" he yelled, barely able to catch his breath. The way she was riding him, like he enjoyed doing to her when he was on top, he prayed this wouldn't be over too fast. A spark flew through him as Gabby writhed wildly over him. With her hands braced on his shoulders, he prayed his lucky chair would hold them and the weight of their loving.

He watched her face. She was close. Dammit, so was he.

"Oh my, oh my, oh my!" Gabby screamed.

He felt a flush of pleasure like silky goodness coat him, making his pulses into her body even slicker. Her release triggered his. Holding her tighter, Adonis leaned up and placed his face between her breasts. That's where he felt at peace with her; he felt at home. He screamed his pleasure at the top of his lungs as she continued to ride him.

Minutes went by before either of them spoke or moved. The sound of loud breathing was all the sound they needed to soothe them.

"Woman! You tried to kill me!" he exclaimed while struggling to breathe evenly.

"It's your fault. You are the one who initiated me into the pleasures of sex. You can't think to turn it off now. I do believe riding you is my favorite position," she said, covering his face with kisses.

"Any position that has me inside of you is my favorite one; any and all of them."

"And you had the nerve to ask me if I was going back to my place when Victoria gets here."

Adonis chuckled out loud.

"I am apologizing for that now. She's flying in on Wednesday? I can get Ray to have someone from his team pick her up," he said.

"Can I pick her up? You were having my truck brought here tomorrow anyway. Plus, she's coming at night. The tags have already been changed on it. No one will know it's me. I need to get back to some regular movements. If I don't, we'll never know if the threat is over. It's been quiet for weeks. Besides, this guy is probably someone who lives back east. It was during my shows on the east coast when I got the most communication from him. There has been nothing since I arrived here. I'll go right to the airport and come back. I'm supposed to have lunch with Jordan on Wednesday also. I can go by myself. You know how tight his security is. I always park in the underground garage that's not open to the public. The elevator goes right to his office. When I leave, it will be the same. Straight to my truck and to the airport. My truck looks just like every other Range Rover on the streets. If I need you or Ray, I will call immediately. Let's try it and see how it goes. I will be safe. I just want a little air; a little breathing room. I have my big, strong boyfriend to protect me. I feel safe."

He didn't want to say yes. Gabby was right. She'd followed his lead for weeks and she was fine. Her feeling like she's a captive wasn't his answer.

"If you see anything or anyone that looks suspicious, you get away as soon as you can and call me at the same time. We'll play it by ear. I have a meeting with Cypher later that day. For most of that day, I have a follow-up on a debrief with the agency I need to do. I'll do that from the local CIA office. I won't be here for most of the day. If you want to entertain your friend at your condo, you can do that. Make sure you either let Ray know or your own security team know. I feel good about the safety of the building. I know you need your girl time."

"Okay. We'll play it all by ear then. You're good with all this? I don't want you to worry too much."

Adonis pulled her into a kiss that lasted well over a minute.

"I'm not worried. I love you. Looks like we'll both be busy

on Wednesday. Let me know the plan."

"I can do that. I have a plan for the next thirty minutes or so. It involves you washing my back in the shower. You game?"

Adonis hopped up, holding her close.

"Just as you always say to me, say less, baby!"

11

Gabby turned her head left and right, checking herself in her hand-held mirror. As a glam-queen, she needed to confirm that she'd covered her naturally full lips correctly with her favorite lip gloss. After puckering her lips three to four times, she looked across Jordan's desk where he impatiently tapped his fingers. His reaction to her pampering was not new. She returned his smile and put her makeup and mirror away.

"Are you done? You look good. The few people who know you're here don't care. You know my story. I've seen you at your worst," Jordan joked.

"Haha. Don't come for me. It's lip gloss. You're lucky I don't have my entire glam squad with me," Gabby retorted.

"I'm actually surprised you don't. I love this new Gabby. The couple of times I visited you at A.D.'s place, I expected makeup and hair people to fall from the rafters like SWAT team members. You traveling solo is a shocker. I mean – no security either?" he questioned.

Even though he'd brought the subject up an hour ago while they ate an early dinner together, when she didn't respond then, he wouldn't let her off the hook a second time.

When she flipped her hair to the side and raked her fingers through it, he saw her usual reaction to a situation she'd rather avoid.

"If you must know, I didn't need security to come and visit my brother. You spend very little time in Los Angeles now that you are living near, but not in the Governor's mansion in Sacramento. I rack up more air miles than me. I wanted to see you while you were here. Your last trip here, you said it would be your last for a while. I don't get to Sacramento often, so it was now or I would have to wait. I wanted to talk to you about something," she admitted.

"I do like this local office most of all out of all of them that are located across California."

"I figured that out when you didn't sell your L.A. home. Besides, the largest of your teams is here. They get more of your presence than the other locations. I guess Brien does a great job of running this place like a well-oiled machine. I saw him twice today. He's quite the lurker when it comes to you."

"Brien take his job very seriously as my right-hand around this place. Stop changing the subject. Why are you flying solo as if you don't have a care in the world? I get the disguise to fake the average person out. Me and your true fans will know it's you. I don't like you being that careless. There is still a threat out there."

"Jordy, you deal with threats every single day. I've seen you without your security team around."

"No, you haven't. You may not see them but they are always close by when I'm not in the security of my office. I'm also not world-known like my baby sister."

"I know. Don't brow-beat me. I got enough of that from Adonis. I promise I'm being safe. I needed to get out of the house for more than rehearsals and studio time. I wanted a little bit of freedom. It's been weeks. I think the major issue is over. I'm only out to see you and to pick up Victoria from the airport. I won't even get out of the truck. Adonis had the tint on my truck windows darkened even more. I hate feeling like I'm caged."

"Yeah, I know you hate it. Comes with the career you've chosen."

"I thought I wanted this."

When Gabby's head dropped and her shoulders slumped, Jordan knew the conversation was about to get deep. Ever since they were kids, the two of them could always talk about everything. When she needed him, even to be an ear, he made time for her. Being the only girl and in a family full of politicians, he tried to let her know that she was a priority.

"You thought? As in the past? What's going on?" he asked.

Jordan leaned back in his large brown leather chair and waited. He liked this local branch, an extension of the governor's office out of Sacramento. When he needed to have a private moment with someone, this is where he came. Brien made sure there weren't any disturbances. His assistant showed up at the door to the office, opening it right after knocking. He and Gabby both looked in Brien's direction.

"Oh, hey again, Gabby. I didn't realize you were still here. I didn't get to speak to you when you arrived. I did wave," he said.

"I waved back. It's always good to see you."

"My pleasure," Brien replied.

A questionable looked covered Jordan's face at the way he noticed Brien was eyeing Gabby. There wasn't a man on earth who didn't look at her that way but Brien was holding his stare uncomfortably long. Jordan cleared his throat.

"Brien? You wanted something?" he asked, bringing his attention to him and away from Gabby.

"Yes, sorry about that. Did you want to extend your time here in L.A. by a few days? Bella is scheduled to be in L.A. tomorrow. She called me saying she's been trying to reach you. I told her you probably forgot your phone in your suit jacket while you were talking with Gabby over a late lunch."

Joran cursed under his breath and reached for his jacket. He'd missed two calls and a few texts from Bella, his girlfriend of the past five years. She was one of the most sought after, hottest models on any runway and they were in love. Knowing she was back from the Paris fashion show and was headed to see him at the home they shared, he was no doubt going to spend a few extra days in town.

"I can't believe I missed her calls. I'll call her. Yes, can you change my flight? Can you check to see if there is anything on my schedule over the next few days that I can't move around? I'd like a few uninterrupted days with Bella."

"I'll do that right away," Brien said.

Jordan kept his eyes on Brien when he didn't back out of the room. Instead, he found his assistant once again eyeing Gabby who wasn't paying attention. She was checking something on her phone and didn't notice. Thinking nothing of it, he pulled his attention away again.

"Do that. Can you make sure I'm not interrupted again while Gabby is here?"

"Oh, sure. You have an important meeting in thirty minutes. Should I postpone that?"

"No, don't do that," Gabby said. "I'll be heading out in about thirty minutes anyway. I want to make a stop at mom and dad's house before I head to the airport to pick up Victoria," she added.

"They're not in town," Jordan said.

"I know. Denali made a special cake for me."

Jordan nodded. He could understand her need to go grab that cake. Denali was their parents' housekeeper. He also prepared their meals when they were in town. He lived full-time in the separate house with its own pool at their house in Calabasas."

"A special cake?" he asked.

"For Adonis," Gabby said and looked toward Brien, who was still in the room.

"That's it, Brien. Anything else?" he asked him.

"No, not at all. I'll make sure you're not disturbed."

Brien finally left, leaving the alone again. Jordan leaned forward with his elbows on his desk top.

"A cake for Adonis? Is this to thank him for looking after you these past weeks by letting you camp out at his place?"

Gabby turned her head toward the door and then back at him. He already knew what this was about. He wanted her to tell him.

"No," she said softly.

"Gabby?"

"How did you know that Bella was the one for you? I mean, how and when did you know that she was the love of your life? I know you're not married. It's been five years. You love her. She loves you. I know you want to marry her. Why her? What was it?" she quizzically asked.

"You know I met her at a rally for my campaign for Mayor. She was already a star model and yet, here she was at my little campaign office lending her support. I watched her work her magic on the room. She had contributors eating out of her hand. I couldn't take my eyes off of her. From that night forward, I never wanted anyone else. We fell in love instantly. She was twenty-five and riding the wave of an incredible career. Yet, here she was lending her support to my campaign. Things were work, work for months. Election night, I asked her out even before word came down that I had won. Then when I was asked to be Lieutenant Governor after a short stint as Mayor, she was right there. When the Governor died and I moved up, she was there breathing life into me all the way. She's been that for me. I've been that for her. That's rare. I wouldn't and couldn't let that go. I do plan to marry Bella. My life is meant to be lived with her. Our hearts were one from the start. Why are you asking me this now?"

"The cake for Adonis? It's not a thank you cake. It's an I love you cake. I want to do something special and romantic. You know I don't cook that well. I do okay when it comes to breakfast food, but not much else. I'm planning to try my hand at cooking a romantic dinner for him. We...are. We are in love, Jordy. Me and Adonis – not just me."

"Oh?"

"Did you know that Adonis had feelings for me that he held back on? I know the two of you are close."

"I did, but not until recently. He only shared that with me after I asked him to check into this threat against you."

"I was so mean to him. I was horrible to him because I thought he stomped on my love for him. He loves me. Adonis, the only man I have ever loved like this also loves me. I could have gone home weeks ago. I haven't. I don't want to. Not ever again. He's my air, Jordy. He's my rock and I am his."

"Sis, I'm not surprised to hear any of this. The two of you

have been foolish for a long time. He had reservations about how being involved with you would impact our family. I made it very clear to him that I will always support your love. It was always meant to be. I'm happy for you."

Gabby nodded and looked over at him. She had more to say.

"We have always been able to talk about anything, right?" she asked.

"Any and everything. That's always been me and you."

"I'm going to get personal. I can with you."

"Yes, you can. Don't overshare, but yes, share," he offered.

"Adonis and I have been intimate."

"I gathered that."

"Okay, but what you may not know is that he was my first."

"Your first? You mean you have been with him before now? What? Years ago?" he asked.

"No. I'm saying, until a few weeks ago, I was still a virgin."

Jordan threw his hands up in surrender. Gabby was sharing much more than he wanted her to.

"Sis."

"I know. You don't want to hear this. I'm saying it to say – that's how serious I was about wanting Adonis and only him."

"Listen, I'm going to share something with you, since we're pouring our hearts out and stuff," he quipped.

"What? You're a virgin too?" Gabby jested.

They both laughed out loud before he could continue.

"You and Adonis are a lot like me and Bella. Our stories are similar in that way."

"Bella was?"

"She was. She told me that she had promised that she

would be until she met her perfect man."

"That's you. Like Adonis is for me."

"Yes. So even though I am surprised of what you just told me, I'm also not so surprised. I've never doubted how you felt about him. Perhaps, back then wasn't the right time. I do believe now is. You seem different. I know the stage and lights has been your life, but there were times when I questioned your happiness in being there. These past few weeks, you are definitely content and happy with life. You're preparing for your show next week. Usually, you would be out painting the town. You not doing so has nothing to do with the threat that's out there. It has to do with what you and Adonis have found at the same time; love. I'm happy for you both."

"I love my career. I'm thankful for it. I know I can have my career and Adonis. I have obligations that have me under contract for these final shows. After that, I'm taking a break. Adonis will only be around for a few more months before he has to set off on a case somewhere in the world. I want this time with him. I need him to know that I'm here now and I will be while he's gone. Every time he returns, I want the first person that he sets eyes on to be me. I want to be his peace, his love. Am I wrong for wanting to give up so much for a man? Am I that woman that people talk about? What does it say about me that I have this man and he's mine and then all I want to do is be in his arms around the clock. We talk about everything. We pop popcorn and watch movies like an old married couple. We swim on the beach. We lay out on his patio, each of us with a book in our hands. There's more but I won't make you crazy by hearing about my love life, now that I have one. I want this. I want him. Right now, that's enough for me."

"Gabby, you are young. You have a lifetime of singing and having the career you want. You can only live your life for you. I don't want you to care about what anyone thinks about your choices. You only have this one life to live. Have the life you want. If it's Adonis, go for it. If it's him and a career – do that too. You can do it all. Just be happy."

"I am happy; I am now. I didn't know I wasn't until now. My priorities are changing. I want to make choices that make my heart flutter. Adonis has the kind of career that will take him away from me at any given time. When he's home, I want to be his home. When he's away, I can focus on my career and making a home for him. I want that. I want what mom and dad have. I want what you and Bella will have. I need what Chad has. I want babies. I want Adonis."

"Sounds to me like you have Adonis. Mom and dad know?"

"They're coming to town soon. I did talk to mom and told her a little. I'll tell them when they arrive."

"They're going to be happy. You know that, right? They have always loved A.D. like a son. They will love him for you."

"I believe so too. Adonis is nervous."

"He'll be fine."

"I wanted you to know what was going on. I saw the questionable looks the few times you came by his house to check on me."

"I could see the way the two of you looked at each other. I'm here for it all. Be careful driving out to the house. Is Victoria's flight late-night?"

"It's in three hours which is why I need to get going. Thanks for lunch or dinner, depending on the way you look at the clock."

Gabby stood and he came around the table and pulled her into a tight hug.

"Be careful. Don't make any detours that Adonis doesn't know about. He'll be worried, I'm sure."

"I'm going to call him while I'm on my way to the house. I'll call you later? Tell Bella I said hello. I miss her. I need to connect with her while she's home."

"She'll love that."

Gabby turned and reached for the handle of his office door and then stopped with her back to him.

"Jordy, I have never been this happy before in my life. It hasn't been a long life at twenty-six. Being in love this much is amazing. I wouldn't change anything."

"And you shouldn't. Only do so based on you and only you. I'm glad that you finally found your way to A.D. I'm looking forward to all those babies!"

**

Brien moved away from the door when he couldn't stand to hear anymore. Gabby had been faking everything about her life with Leo. That was the man he thought he had to worry about. Now he hears that she's in love with someone named Adonis. Who was that? His mind raced and he walked back to his office and gathered his things. He couldn't handle another bit of work today. He couldn't focus on anything other than who this man was that Gabby was in love with. Hearing that she's been sleeping with this guy and that he was her first made him fiercely angry. Now that he knew that Gabby had been a virgin all this time, he knew that she was meant to be his. She wasn't meant to give her body to anyone other than him. The fact that she didn't, pissed him off.

"Ugh!" he breathed harshly. "That bitch!" he screamed.

Brien covered his mouth. He had to remember that he was in the office and a yell as loud as that could be heard by anyone. He had to maintain his cool.

Looking at the time, he knew that Jordan would be heading into a meeting in the next few minutes. That would mean that Gabby was on her way out. She would be alone. When he arrived, he was just as surprised as Jordan had been that she wasn't surrounded by a group of muscled men. He had secretly waited for a time like this where nothing would be in his way of getting to her. If Jordan was going to his meeting, he could have a chance to connect with Gabby while she was still in the building.

He hustled around his office snatching up his suit jacket and his phone. Gabby would no doubt take the elevator closest to Jordan's office to the garage since that was the only elevator that wasn't for others in the office. Only he and Jordan used that elevator.

Pacing around before he walked out, he knew he needed a plan. Snapping his fingers, he had the perfect idea. Jordan's birthday was coming up. She wouldn't be able to say no to his proposal. He only needed her undivided attention.

Leaving his office and heading toward Jordan's he knew how to get it. Gabby would never see her lover again. He would see to that. She was his now and forever. It was time he proved that to her.

12

Brien didn't care about consequences anymore. He was in a perfect position to get Gabby to finally notice him. He has spent over a year of his life trying to get her in line. Showing her that she needed a strong man in her life to protect her was his life's work. His anger rose to an unimaginable level at the thought that she'd been giving herself to an old crush. How could he have missed that part of her life?

He assumed he'd learned everything about her by snooping around her brother's life. Being the first executive assistant to Jordan, even before he became governor, gave him access to her that not many others had. Something was changing. There was a chill in the air between him and Jordan of late. If by chance Jordan was becoming aware of his prying eyes and ears, he needed to act faster than he'd planned. The way Jordan watched him when he stepped into his office in the middle of his talk with Gabby, he was left with his own unsettling feeling. He should have known better than to focus on Gabby in such close quarters. He couldn't help himself. He was so close to her that he could have reached out and touched her.

Jordan trusted him with everything, except where Gabby was now staying and who she was with. There was a mystery guy shielding her from him and he was getting tired of it. He thought putting fear in Gabby in every city except for the one where he lived would be his answer to get her back to Los Angeles for good. He wanted her running scared to the only safe haven left available to her; her home.

A few times over the past few months, he was able to strike up a conversation with her. He hated that his engagements with her seemed forced. It was clear she wasn't interested in him. That wouldn't stop him from planting himself in or near Jordan's office every time she was around, like today. He wanted her to feel safe around him so that she'd be more apt to let her guard down. If he hadn't been this obsessed with a woman before, he wouldn't be as comfortable knowing his plan would work. The mistakes of the past would not come up again. Having Gabby was too important to him. She was all that he ever wanted and needed in life.

Stalking her condo hadn't produced much. She hadn't been there since the first night of her return. She had entered her building flanked by a man he couldn't get a good look at. It had to be this Adonis person he heard Jordan and Gabby talking about as he eavesdropped on their conversation. As he thought back, that could have been the guy she as sleeping with. He'd been lucky enough to know she was returning that day. He'd planned everything out perfectly. He was able to acquire the key to Gabby's condo by stealing Jordan's copy and making his own copy. He then returned Jordan's before he knew he'd had it.

Hours before her plane landed, he'd gone to her place to set it up for a night of romance. He was going to finally make his move by showing her how much he loved and adored her. She may find it creepy at first that he would have been inside of her place, but through his love and devotion, which he planned to lay on thick, he had a feeling any sensation of uneasiness would go away once he shared how much he was willing to sacrifice to have her.

Leaving her place after making sure the scene was set for their love, he waited across the street from the entrance. He grew angry when she didn't show up at all. His first try of getting to her was a bust when a sleek black truck pulled up. He grew anxious expecting her. He was ready. Gabby never stepped out of the truck. Instead, there were several guys who hopped out of the truck and raced through the front entrance of her condo. Something was wrong. Why wasn't she with them? He later found out that they were sent to check out her place before she arrived to be sure it was safe. The next day, he overheard Jordan explaining that to his father.

He returned the next day, not really sure why. After what he knew had been discovered, there would be no reason for her to arrive. Then he realized, she still may arrive, but with security. She probably wasn't going to stay in a place that someone could easily have access to.

His next thought was that she would be staying with Jordan. Though he was living full-time in Sacramento, he still kept his place in Los Angeles and came home anytime he had a few days of no appointments on his calendar.

As luck would have it, Gabby did show up that second day. This time with that mysterious man. They spent very little time in her place. When they exited, the man was carrying several large suitcases. His face was still hidden as they got into the back of the truck they arrived in. He tried to follow them to see where she was going. Due to some great maneuvering by the driver, he lost them about two miles after turning his own truck around to get behind them.

His mind reminisced about all the times he wished he could be this close to Gabby. He listened passionately to her as she explained to him her own ideas about the party he told her he wanted to host for Jordan.

Excitement shot through him knowing that tonight was his last chance. Gabby surprised him by showing up at Jordan's office and staying as long as she did. It wasn't until after her visit was over that he finally got the chance to talk to her. His timing couldn't have been more perfect. Best of all, he'd seen her truck. She'd arrived alone. The best idea he'd had was to pull back on terrorizing her. She was back to feeling free. Thankfully, he was quick on his feet. He saw her leaving and had to think of a story. The party was the perfect ploy. If he could convince her to plan it with him, that would put them even closer together. When she agreed to meet him to talk about the party for Jordan he was thrilled. This was the perfect gateway to his plan.

Catching up to her at the elevator, she explained that she had a few hours before she had to pick up her friend. He told her of an out of the way restaurant where they could go and talk. They drove a few blocks in their own cars to a small place that didn't get a lot of people patronizing it. He tried to convince her to ride with him. He offered to bring her back, but something in her demeanor told him that he was pressing too hard too soon. He was here. She was here. He was cruising high on this train ride of luck.

Sitting across the table from her, he was nervous. This was the first time he'd ever been alone with her. The feeling gave him a thrill he never expected. He was imagining spending years and years across a table from her just like this. They would be happily married with three or four beautiful children who looked just like her. He would be at the height of his career as a politician. His ultimate goal was to make her the country's first lady. First, he had to clean up her flashy lifestyle. She would no longer need to perform and show her body to millions of men who gawked and clawed at her. He wished he could have talked her into dinner to make their time together seem more like a date, but she only wanted a glass of lemonade and a slice of sweet potato pie. He smiled through his discontent at her lack of living in the moment with him and not on the outside of it as if he really only wanted to be in her presence to talk about a party. He liked Jordan a lot. In fact, the man was his hero. He looked forward to the day that he'd be able to call him his brother-in-law.

"Brien, all of your ideas for a party for Jordan are great. Let's talk again about it real soon. I need to get going so that I'm not late," Gabby said.

The reality of what was about to happen hit him. She was leaving. He'd wasted time thinking about being with her instead of laying on his charm.

He noticed a nervousness to her voice. Something about him changed her interaction with him and he didn't like it. By now, he had hoped to have her eating out of his hands. He wanted her falling for him the way he'd fallen for her. He wasn't ready for her to leave. Without thinking, he reached across the table and placed his hand over hers. When she attempted to move her hand, he gripped her in a tighter grasp.

"Please don't leave yet. I was hoping after all this party stuff that you and I could maybe go out and spend some time together. You know, I've admired you for a long time. I've been to several of your concerts in other states. One time, I flew out of here in the morning and caught a red-eye flight back after the show. You were amazing. You sing from your heart and I love that."

"Um, Brien, are you asking me out?"

He could feel her shivering. She was frightened. He saw it in her demeanor. He didn't care. What he knew for sure was that Gabby wasn't going anywhere without him. He smiled hoping to calm her fear. She looked terrified. She had on dark glasses and a baseball cap that covered her face so that she wouldn't be seen. Still, he saw all of her.

"Well, yeah. I think we could make a good couple. You're beautiful. I know everything about you already. You just need time to get to know me."

"You know everything about me? How? What do you know?" she asked.

"I've been working for your brother a long time. He talks about you all the time."

"Brien, let go of my hand. Do you realize you're squeezing it kind of tight? In fact, my fingers are starting to hurt," she said to him while looking around. To him, it appeared that she was looking for someone to step in. Was she looking for help? Against him? He didn't want to hurt her. He wanted to love her.

He laughed it off. He was being too anxious.

"Sorry about that. I got lost in your beautiful eyes for a minute and wasn't thinking. Like I was saying, maybe we can have dinner one day this week after Victoria flies back to New York. That's where she's living now, right? I know y'all grew up together here in L.A. I follow her on IG."

"You follow Victoria?" she asked.

Brien heard her voice tremble.

"Well, yeah. I follow you too but not just on IG, but on all of your social media platforms. Would it be too much to ask you to follow me back? I see that you follow some people. I'd like to be in that number. You never know. Once we go out on our first date and I amaze you with my charming personality, you'll want to be able to keep up with me on social media. I want to be able to tag you in pictures of us together. Imagine that. Me in love with Gabrielle Mann and she in love with me."

"Brien, I'm seeing someone," she stammered out.

His heart stopped. He didn't want to hear her say it again. Maybe he could get more information on the guy and illuminate his competition. He played as if he didn't know.

"What? Who? I don't see anything serious on your social media. Jordan never speaks of you with anyone. Are you talking about Leo? Everyone knows that's just for show to build both of your careers. I'm not threatened by him. Besides, I hope you realize he really does have hoes in every area code," he joked.

When he laughed by himself, he felt silly. Gabby looked like she'd seen a ghost.

"Listen, I'm going to go. I'll call you about the party stuff," she said standing to leave.

"Will you?" he asked sidling up to her.

"Will I what?" she asked sternly.

"Call me. You have my number? If not, I can text it to your phone. Look, I'm sending it to you right now."

"You have my number?" she asked.

"Of course. I work for your brother," he said walking behind her as she suddenly started moving away from him.

As her steps quickened so did his. He followed her through the door and out into the parking lot. He saw her looking around just as he was doing. To his delight, they were in the lot by themselves. He was happy they couldn't be seen by anyone, even those in the restaurant. Now was the time to make his move. He had all they would need in several bags he packed and placed in the back of his truck. If she went willingly, he would happily give her the big red duffle bag he packed of things in her size that he thought she would like. If not, the gray bag was for his use. She wouldn't like what he had in it.

Brien's pulse raced when Gabby started walking faster.

"I already told you I'm seeing someone."

"But I just told you about Leo and his women. You don't really want him. He doesn't deserve you and this beautiful vessel. Or is there someone else? I heard you talking to Jordan. Who is Adonis? Is that the man you're giving yourself to? I have to tell you, I don't like it. I know I sound crazy, but I have so little time to let you know that I've actually been in love with you for a long time."

When Gabby reached her truck and searched for her key fob, he knew she was trying to get away from him. Why do women treat him like that after he confesses his love for them? Gabby had to want him like he wanted her.

"I really have to go, Brien."

He walked up so close to her that the move pinned her to the driver's side door of her truck. His body was pressed up against hers. Years and years, he'd prayed to be this close to her and now he was here. Her hair smelled like lavender. Her body essence smelled like soft wild flowers.

"I don't like thinking about other men touching you. I wrote that to you a million times. I told you what I would do if you let any man touch you; you're mine. I understand that you don't have feelings for me yet, but it will grow over time. I have a perfect place I've purchased in the mountains where we can live off the grid together; just you and me."

Gabby squirmed to try and get away from him. He felt her body shiver against his. He reached and turned her around to face him. He was no longer playing. This was his only chance and he was taking it.

"Stop it Brien. You're hurting me. Are you out of your mind? Are you crazy?" she screamed.

"Do *NOT* shout at me or call me crazy! I've been building a life for us for years. I worked hard to get you back here to California so that you were near me. Didn't my letters explain how serious I am about you? I know you read them before turning them over to the police. I'm not trying to hurt you, Gabby. I love you. I love you to death – either mine or yours. I will not let you reject me like other women have. I've put a lot of time and energy into knowing everything there is to know about you. So much time has been wasted already," he said grabbing onto her hand to keep her from pressing the button to open her truck.

He knew if she were able to get into it, she would get away from him. He couldn't go back now. He'd made his move. He'd revealed who he truly was. She would go running right to her brother or perhaps the police. He couldn't have that. He only needed time to prove to her that she could love him as deeply as he loved her. If not, he would happily die together with her. They would surely be together in eternity.

"You? The letters? Those were you? You are insane. Get away from me!" she yelled.

Brien reached to cover her mouth in an attempt to silence her. When he tried to hold her tight in his grip to move her closer to his truck, a pain unlike any he'd ever experienced before surfaced through him. It started in his groin and raced throughout his body. Somehow, Gabby had caught him off guard with a knee to his groin. The pain was deafening to everything else happening around him. He tumbled over to the ground. Gabby dropped her keys. He tried to reach for them as he writhed around in pain. With the strength of what felt like a sumo wrestler, she stomped down on his outstretched hand while the other hand still covered his groin. He yelped like a wild animal after her second stomp. Fully engulfed in the pain that was now slamming into his brain, he couldn't stop her when she grabbed her keys and raced the few steps to her truck. He heard her start up her truck as he screamed her name. He yelled for her to come back to him or he would kill her. She heard him. He saw pure fear on her face. That's not what he wanted to see. Since she'd chosen violence, as soon as he could move, he would answer the same way. It was clear she didn't want him. She wasn't submitting to him the way that he wanted. He still wanted her but now, he had to make sure she either came with him or she would die in front of him.

His eyes followed her truck as it peeled out of the parking lot. He noted the direction she took on Pacific Coast Highway. With the little strength he had, he crawled to his own truck and managed to get himself up into it. As he continued to wince in pain as sweat pour from his face as if he'd run a marathon, he put his truck in drive and raced off after her.

While driving, he dialed her phone. She ignored him. As he turned onto the highway in pursuit of her, he screamed at his phone to call the love of his life. That was how he had her listed on his phone. Again, and again, he called her. Each time the call went unanswered. He sat up as straight as he could. He needed to concentrate on Gabby and not on the pain. He had to get to her before she got to anyone else. If she did, his life was over. When he had planned to gradually ease her into a date, hearing that she was seeing someone had him seeing fire. He'd heard her say it earlier to Jordan, but to hear her say it to him cut him deep. There was a mystery person loving his woman. He would never let that happen again.

"I see you," he shouted, growling at her though she couldn't hear him.

Up ahead, he saw her truck weaving in and out of traffic. He needed to stop her before a cop spotted her. Then he would need to go in a different direction to not be caught. At this point, he was surely going to jail. Getting closer to her, he pulled up alongside her speeding truck. Not caring about the impact of his next move, he swerved his truck to the right and slammed into the back side of her truck. He couldn't let her get away. He shouted at her through the closed window. His other hand was still holding onto his crotch, preventing him from rolling down the window. His actions told her that he wanted her to pull over. When he continued to race forward with cars honking at them as they sped down the highway, he kept up with her. There was no going back now. She was pissing him off. He's a nice guy. He would do anything for her. He loved her like no other man could ever love her. She would make a perfect wife while also giving him the most beautiful kids. That's what he thought about, causing him to smile a little. So many thoughts raced through his mind. He wondered if this is what life was like in the head of his crazy brother, Dustin.

Speeding up, he rammed into her truck in the back

causing her truck to sway from side to side. Still, she continued on, driving faster.

"Okay, if this is your answer – remember you chose!" he shouted, determined to stop her.

Getting his bearings, he focused. It looks like they were about to have a Romeo and Juliet kind of ending. He was ready to die for her.

13

Adonis couldn't seem to catch his breath. There were several times in his career when this has happened to him before. Those were times when something wasn't quite right. This was one of those times. He'd been concerned about Gabby being out on her own all day. He made her a promise that he wouldn't smother her. He was going to stick to that. If something were wrong, she knew how to reach him. The fact that he reached for his phone more than once in the past few minutes to make sure it was working proved he was on edge.

Pulling out of the garage of the local CIA office where he'd just gotten out of a meeting, he made a dash for the expressway. His plan was to go home to whip up some kind of dinner. A night of romance was top on his list. Never had he been this focused on loving a woman. He already knew the reason was that there hadn't been a Gabby in his life before she was; at least, not in the loving way that she was now. He also wondered how much loving they would be able to get in knowing her friend was coming for a visit. He would make enough for him, Gabby and Victoria, just in case they come back to the house. Gabby having her freedom to live her life was important to him.

His thoughts were startled when his phone rang. He answered Cypher's call through the dashboard of his truck.

"Hey brother," he said immediately.

"Where have you been? I've been calling you for over an hour."

Adonis heard the rushed tone of his voice. Something was wrong.

"At the CIA office here in L.A. You know when we're inside, our phones are put away during a briefing. I just turned it on the minute I left the building."

"Have you talked to Gabby?" Cypher quickly asked.

"I was about to send her a text to check on her. She went to see her brother. From there, she was going to head to pick up a friend from the airport. What's going on?" Adonis asked.

"I think I have made some headway that you'll appreciate. You tell me what you think about it. You asked me to take a closer look into the people who are closest to Gabby. The Leo fella is clean as a whistle. He's a dog when it comes to women. I'm glad your lady never got involved with him for more than camera purposes."

Adonis breathed a huge sigh of relief. He'd been saying the same to himself for weeks.

"Tell me about it. There have been times when I wanted to kill him when I saw him getting a little too close to her. I'm aware that feeling this way was for naught."

Adonis laughed off how silly he'd been acting out of jealousy.

"I've gone down the list of people from her photographer, makeup people, dancers, executives – pretty much everyone. There is nothing there. There is something I need you to think long and hard over. The guy who works for Gabby's brother,

Brien. He's high on my list."

"What!" Adonis yelled.

"Hear me out. I've discovered a glitch in who he is. Well, that is who he has been recently. Brien has a brother who has been in a mental facility most of his adult life. His name is Dustin. When I looked into Brien's life, I discovered that there are traces of his brother being out and traveling to various places around the country. Each time, they coincide with one of Gabby's shows. Have you ever heard of this Dustin fella?"

"No, never. We can ask Jordan."

"We'll get to that next. He will most likely say no. I say that because, though I have Dustin outside of the facility, my contact is quite sure that he has never left the facility. In fact, he's in a maximum-security part of the place for their most dangerous residents."

Adonis shook his head from side to side in disbelief.

"How is that possible?"

"What do you know about Brien? Anything other than he works for Jordan?" Cypher asked.

"Nothing at all. Jordan raves about the great work he's done for him over the past few years. I've never been around him. I keep lowkey around outsiders."

"I get that," Cypher noted.

Jordan pulled his truck off at the next exit and sped into a nearby parking lot. He needed to think while they talked. He couldn't do that and focus on the road at the same time.

"Talk to me," Adonis said, trying to calm himself.

"Of everyone I looked into, the only person that gave me a reason to question them is this Brien guy. Something strange is up with him. Do you know if he always travels with Jordan? Has he ever shown any interest in Gabby?"

"I don't know. I would need to talk to Jordan about that. Let me connect him. Hold tight."

Adonis quickly dialed Jordan and added him to the call.

"A.D." Jordan answered immediately.

"Jordan, listen, do you have a minute? Is Gabby still with you?" Adonis asked hastily.

"Yeah, I have a minute. I'm headed into a meeting, but there is always time for you. Gabby left about thirty minutes ago. What's happening?" Jordan asked.

"Listen, I have a friend on the line. You can call him Cypher. I asked him to do some background checks for me into those closest to Gabby. To be completely transparent here, I also asked him to look into a few people that are close to people who are close to Gabby. That means those closest to you."

"Okay, I get that," Jordan acknowledged. "As long as we find the threat, you should look under every rock at everyone."

"I'm glad you agree," Cypher said joining the conversation. "Jaguar has talked about you a lot over the years. I'm glad to finally meet you. Should I call you Adonis? We don't usually, but it's just the three of us," he added.

"Jordan is one of four people who know my code name. That number includes his parents and now Gabby. We're good," Adonis said.

"Cypher, A.D. has mentioned you as well. He speaks highly of the times you've saved him on one mission or another. He's my brother. I appreciate you for that. Tell me what's going on," Jordan said.

"How far back into Brien's life has your background checks gone over the years? I know you've done them or should I say, had them done for everyone you employ consider the nature of your work in politics. How thorough?" Cypher asked.

"Very thorough."

"So, you know about his brother?"

"Dustin? Yes, I know about him. He's been in a facility since around age fifteen – a lot of years. He and Brien are two years apart. I don't think Brien gets to see him much. He's in a place in Colorado or something like that. What's all of this questioning about?"

"According to what I've been able to dig up, Dustin, or someone claiming to be Dustin has been flying all over the country. The most concerning is that Dustin's identification has been used for plane tickets and most importantly, for the purchase of tickets to your sister's shows. I mean, lots of her shows this year alone. Is Brien always traveling with you?"

"No. He doesn't travel with me often. He overseas my local office here in Los Angeles."

"Has Brien ever talked about being at any of Gabby's shows?"

"Wait!" Adonis jumped in.

"Yeah," Cypher said. "The floor is yours."

"I can't believe I let this go by me without a second thought. Gabby said she thought she saw Brien at a few of her shows. Most recently, she was out at a club a few weeks back when she first arrived back in town. She swears she saw him in the crowd. When she looked back the first time, he tried to hide his face. She looked again after being distracted and he was gone."

"How sure was she?" Jordan asked.

"Very sure but then she let it go saying it couldn't have been him. Yes, she thought she saw him at shows in different locations, too. If he was the person she saw at her shows, that would mean he would be flying around the country while still being in Los Angeles," Adonis answered. "He can't be in two places at the same time."

"Guys, today while Gabby was here, Brien kept coming up with reasons to interrupt my time with her. Something seemed odd when she was in my office. The way he looked at her made me feel strange. His eyes were claiming her in a weird way. He interrupted my lunch with her two times. He just kept coming back. Then when we were in my office, he found reasons to come by though he could have waited. He was nervous. Quite fidgety, actually. It was odd."

"I don't want either of you to fly off the handle, but I think Brien has been using identification and even credit cards in his brother's name. That's how he's able to get in and out of L.A. without there being a trail. There are social media accounts under Dustin's name. Every single image and video are of Gabby out and about or at one of her shows. I think Brien is your stalker. He's been publicly living as Brien, but privately, he is his brother. They look so much alike, it's scary. Jordan, do you know where Brien is right now? Gabby was there when he was?" Cypher asked.

"Yes, she was. No, I don't know where Brien is. He was supposed to be at my last meeting, which only lasted about twenty minutes. He was a no-show. I called him just now about my next meeting and he didn't pick up."

"Shit!" Adonis yelled. "Where is Gabby? Would he have been able to get to her as she was leaving?"

"Hold up! I saw him and Gabby talking at the elevator as I was heading to my meeting. I assumed he was on his way to the meeting and stopped to chat her up for a few minutes. One second," Jordan said.

Adonis heard the line click as if Jordan put them on hold.

"Why didn't I figure this out? I've been so busy loving her that I slipped up. I usually pick up on weird behavior," Adonis said.

"Not if you're not around him," Cypher said.

"But Gabby said she thought she saw him. I should have looked into that."

"Don't do this. Keep calm and let's talk this out. In the meantime, we need to find Gabby."

"Guys?" Jordan said. "I had my assistant try to reach Brien and she was told he left the building. No one has heard from him for almost an hour. His phone is off. He's never done that before."

"I've been dialing Gabby on my other cell and her phone goes right into her voicemail. I've got to find her. If Brien has his hands on her, he is dead! Do you hear me? He's already dead. Badge or not, I will kill him."

"Jaguar, I can track her truck."

"I'm sending you the information on her truck right now. You do that. Jordan, where was Gabby going when she left?" Adonis asked.

"Out to my parents' house. She was going there to pick up a cake or something. From there, she was going to pick up Victoria at LAX."

"That's what she told me too. Why isn't she answering her phone? I'm hitting the road. It's dark out, so it will be harder with all of this evening traffic. Jordan, can you find out if she's at your parents' house? In the meantime, Cypher, when you have pinged her location, send me the coordinates immediately. We have to find my woman. I mean, right now!"

Adonis yelled before ending the call.

He pressed his foot to the gas pedal and the truck lurched forward. Jumping back on the highway, he set his phone to keep dialing Gabby. Even though it never rang, but went right into her voicemail, he let the dialing continue. That was the only way to feel close to her while his nerves were shot to hell. The only thing that mattered to him right this moment was finding Gabby. If need be, killing Brien if even a hair on Gabby's body is out of place. Brien will wish for the day when he never knew the name Gabby Mann.

With one phone on speed dial to Gabby, he called Ray with the other. One of them had to find themselves closest to Gabby once he was able to reach her.

**

Gabby couldn't breathe. How could she have placed herself in this kind of danger? She should have known something was off the moment Brien walked up to her at the elevator. He'd been acting strange since she arrived at Jordan's office.

With Adonis taking care of some business, she felt free being out from under constant watch since she'd gotten back to town. Even though Adonis would be mad that she was planning on one detour, she struck out on her own since she was going straight to see Jordan when she left the house. Not telling him about her second stop turned out to be her first mistake of the day. The second had been forgetting to power up her cell phone. Her third was trusting Brien. She hadn't read the signs clearly.

She'd never driven so fast or wildly before. She was so focused on getting away from Brien, that it didn't occur to her to call the police or Adonis. She now remembered that while she as with Brien, her phone had died. She hadn't plugged it in the night before. When Adonis arrived that evening, shortly after she had arrived from another rehearsal at the studio, she fell into his arms. That's all she had on her mind. She forgot she'd let the power on her phone dwindle throughout the day.

She was having a hard time trying to keep her truck from crashing into anyone else while she fumbled to connect her phone to her car's power.

After Brien terrorized her with the second hit to her truck, she found a crowd of cars to get ahead of, putting a little distance between them. That gave her a few seconds to connect her phone with a free hand. It took a few seconds, but then the screen lit up as she placed it on the stand in the cup holder. She yelled at her phone to call Adonis. In seconds, his face appeared on the screen. He answered on the first ring.

"A.D.!" she screamed.

"Gabby, baby, where are you? I've been calling you for the past ten minutes or so. Why was your phone off? Where are you?"

"A.D., help me!" she screamed.

"Baby, what's going on? What's with all the horn honking? Talk to me. Is it Brien? Is he nearing you?" he asked.

"Yes! You know about him? He's trying to run me off the road. I think he's trying to kill me after I rejected him. He's been sending me those notes and letters. It's him! I didn't know," she screamed as a rush of adrenaline pumped through her.

She reached up and wiped the tears from her eyes that flowed like a faucet. Her vision was blurry from them. She could only think about being home in Adonis' arms. She knew safety was there. Regret of going out alone set in quickly.

"I know. I'm trying to find you. The cops are trying to find you. Where are you? I'm coming to you. Are you in your truck?"

"Yes!"

"What's Brien in? Take your time and focus. How fast are you driving?"

"Pretty fast. I'm doing ninety-five right now. I can't go slower or he'll catch up. He's already rammed into me twice. Should I pull over somewhere?" she hollered.

Gabby's eyes darted about. She tried to watch the traffic while also keeping her eye on Brien's car approaching quickly in her rearview mirror.

"No, baby. As much as I want you to, you can't stop. I don't know how far from you I am to get to you before he gets to you if you stop driving. I know it's dangerous, but focus and tell me where you are. Are you close to my house on the PCH? Look around."

"Ah! He hit the back of my truck again. No one is helping!" he cried.

"Baby, that's the way of this world right now. Face what's happening and talk to me. I have to find you. Stay on the phone with me."

"I'm not a stunt driver. I'm scared I will hit someone," she cried.

"I know. Stay focused on my voice. You can't see me, but you can hear me. I know you're scared. I am too. Let's do this together," Adonis urged.

Gabby nodded her head as if he could see her. She kept her eyes on the road and both hands on the steering wheel. She needed to be able to control the truck if Brien were able to hit her again.

"Okay," she said, hearing the sound of her voice. She was

scaring herself.

"Cypher, where is she?"

She could hear Adonis talking. She knew who Cypher was. He was one of the guys who worked with him as an agent. She'd heard the name many times before.

"Adonis?" she hollered.

"Baby, I'm getting your location. Keep your eyes on the road and drive. Do not leave that highway for any reason. According to Cypher, you're headed toward me. I'm about three miles apart from you. I'm in my truck driving like a bat out of hell. I'm coming, baby. I'm coming straight to you. I'm in my truck. You know what it looks like. I will signal when I see you by flashing my lights at you. When you see that and see me, I need you to try and safely pull off of the road. I'm going to cut Brien off. He still behind you?"

"Yes," she continued to cry.

"I got you, baby. You're doing good. Keep driving. I'm already flashing my lights. Let me know when you see me. Ray is coming at you from behind Brien. He just sent me a message saying he's close to him."

"I'm scared," she cried out louder.

"I know you are. Listen to my voice and concentrate. I'm trying to remain calm. I need you to do the same thing. He's not going to get to you. I'll kill him first."

"Baby!" she called out to him.

"I got you."

"I see flashing lights. Is that you? I can see some lights coming at me flashing really fast."

An excitement ran through Gabby. She tried to focus on what he told her to do once she saw him. She struggled to remember. Her eyes were on not causing an accident.

"That's me. Ray says he's right behind Brien. You're a few cars away from him. That will give me some room to slide between you and cut him off."

"He'll run into you. No, A.D., don't do that. He could kill you."

"Oh, it's not my death you need to worry about. If I get my hands on him, it's over for him. I do this kind of stuff for a living. I know what to do. Flash your lights, sweetheart," Adonis exclaimed.

Gabby did just that as she saw his truck coming closer.

"Okay, slow a little and pull into the large lot to your right. After you turn, come to a complete stop in the lot. I'm going to swerve in front of Brien. He may hit me, but my truck can handle the impact."

"Okay," she replied nervously. She had to trust that he knew what he was doing. He wasn't just any agent. His name was, Jaguar.

"I see Brien. I see him! Son of a bitch. I need to ram his truck. Trust me that I'll be okay. Pull off and stay in that truck. Unless it's smoking, do not get out until I get to you!"

Before she could answer, the call disconnected. Gabby saw the lot. She saw Adonis waving her off the road. Her eyes captured his every move even as she took a sharp right, cutting cars off as she veered off the road. With her heart beating like a huge drum in her chest, she watched as Adonis moved his truck into the very center of the road between traffic going in both directions. He was about to hit Brien's truck head-on. In the next second, the loud sound of metal smashing into metal pierced the air. It wasn't from Adonis hitting Brien's truck. Instead, she held her breath and watched as Ray's big green truck sped up as Adonis moved out of the way. She didn't know what kind of secret messaging they had going on, but they were in sync.

Ray hit Brien's truck in such a way to cause it to spin out of control. Brien's truck slammed into a large light pole head-on. The loud crash was like a sonic boom on a quiet night. Cars going in every direction avoided collisions. With Brien's truck impaled on the pole, Gabby finally pulled her truck to a stop. She watched Adonis jump out of his truck and head straight for Brien. Her eyes darted to Ray who was also out of his truck and heading toward Brien. Gabby knew what was coming next. If Ray didn't stop Adonis, she knew the plan that he would put on Brien and she didn't want that. Brien did wrong, yes, but she only cared that Adonis not get himself hurt. She yelled Adonis' name over and over. She wanted to pull his attention away from his threat to kill Brien.

Ray reach Brien before Adonis could get his hands on him. Flashing lights were everywhere as law enforcement finally pulled up to the scene. Ray put himself between Brien and Adonis. He was protecting his friend.

No longer following Adonis' instruction to stay in her truck, she hopped out and ran for him. If she could just get to him everything would be alright.

"Adonis!" she yelled as she raced as fast as she could in five-in heels.

His head spun around as their eyes locked. An even bigger horrific look appeared on his face. She knew why. She was doing her best to avoid getting hit by a car as she raced out onto the PCH, not caring to look in any direction other than at him.

With all that was happening, she only wanted to get to him. Suddenly, his attention turned from Brien to her. He raced in her direction, waving cars off as he ran.

"Baby, stop running. I'm coming to you! Gabby, stop before a car runs into you!" he yelled.

She heard him but couldn't stop.

Nothing he said stopped her. In an instant, he had her in his arms. She gripped his neck tight.

"I got you. Baby, I got you," he crooned against her face. Gabby felt every kiss his planted from her chin to her forehead. She took it all in.

"I got you too," she said.

** **

"Gabby, are you hurt? Baby, did he hurt you in any way? I am going to kill him. You stay here," he said.

"No, no. Don't let me go. He didn't hurt me. Don't kill him. Don't leave me," she cried.

Hearing her wails, Adonis fought the need to take care of Brien. No one hurts his woman and lives. The image of men he'd taken care of for his country hadn't endured anything like what he wanted to release on Brien. Gabby was his priority. Ray and the police were handling Brien.

His eyes darted when he saw several large black trucks with darkly tinted windows speeding before coming to a screeching halt in the midst of the scene.

In the next second, men hopped out at the same time as Jordan. He was looking wildly around, no doubt, looking for Gabby. Adonis called out and waved him over. Jordan started to head in their direction with his security close to him. At the last second, he changed directions and instead, headed toward Brien.

Adonis watched with shock in his eyes as Jordan pummeled Brien relentlessly. No one could hold the governor of California back as he landed one rage-filled punch after another. Adonis forgot the power his friend wielded. After all, they met when they were teammates on the same high-school wrestling team. Jordan, like him, was six-foot-five and all muscle. He was allowed to get a few hits in before he was pulled off of Brien. His assistant was now crying like a wounded puppy. Officers finally jumped in to get cuffs on Brien. Jordan's detail shielded his rage from the public trying to get an eyeful.

"Jordan!" Gabby yelled, pulling his attention away.

This time, her brother did race to them. Adonis still stood with Gabby in his arms. He let her down when Jordan reached her and pulled her close to him.

"Are you alright? I didn't know. I'm sorry, sis. I didn't know."

"I know, Jordy. No one knew. I didn't have a clue when he wanted to talk to me about planning a party with him for you. He got creepy after we talked when I wanted to leave. Things got really scary. I think he was trying to kill me by ramming my truck. I didn't recognize the wild look in his eyes. I've never seen that in him," she explained.

Adonis listened as the words rambled out of her mouth. He knew she was in shock after what happened. He pulled her back close to his body as she talked on with Jordan.

"He fooled us all," Jordan said. "When I think of what could have happened to you," he said.

"Jordan, she's okay, but we need to get her out of here," Adonis said. "This is about to get really crazy. I know she shouldn't leave the scene, but just knowing who she is, the media will have a frenzy. They'll overwhelm her," he added.

Adonis looked for Ray who must have known what was

next. Before he could call for him, Ray was standing in front of him, blocking any view of him from prying eyes.

Jordan then turned to him.

"You need to get out of here too, A.D. You know camera crews are going to show up any minute. You can't be on any of them," Jordan declared.

Adonis had been so focused on Gabby that he forgot all about himself. Jordan was right, he needed to be ghost. He took a moment to breathe and turned to Ray.

"At the end of all of this, get Gabby's truck to the garage at her building. I'm going to have my guy pick it up. Have one of your guys take it there. I don't want a random tow truck getting their hands on it. When word gets out that this is Gabby's truck, things are going to go ballistic. Trent will bring a covered truck to pick it up so that's it's not seen."

He then turned to Gabby.

"Are you hurt? Do you need to go to the hospital? I don't want you in a random ambulance either. Too many eyes and ears," Adonis explained.

"No, I'm fine. I want to go with you," she cried, moving tighter into his embrace.

"Baby, you can't. I have some things I need to do. You have to let me do them. Go home. Ray and his team will not leave your side until I get there. Isn't that right, Ray?" he questioned with one eye on Gabby and then on Ray, looking for reassurance.

"I'm not going anywhere until I see the whites of your eyes, bro," Ray assured him.

"I'll stick around to answer questions. All they will need is Gabby's license plate to then find out it belongs to her; to the family. I'll handle the reporters. I've called my parents. They are out of the country, but on their way back right now. I'll give them an update in a minute," Jordan explained. "I agree. We need to get Gabby's truck out of here."

"Jordan, can I stay with you?" Gabby asked.

"Sis, please go with Ray. Right now, he's the only person outside of A.D. that I would trust with you. If he trusts Ray, then Ray is my new best friend. I know he'll do everything to keep any and every one at bay. I will handle the cops. I don't want you here for the mayhem that's about to happen," Jordan said.

"You'll have your hands full explaining the way you landed those punches on Brien," Adonis said.

"I know. I was targeted on what he could have done to her if you hadn't shown up with Ray. I'm ready to respond to any questions about that. She's my sister before I'm the governor. I don't care what anyone has to say about that," Jordan boldly proclaimed.

More people began showing up. The agent in him told him it was time to leave. He couldn't be caught on any cameras. For now, he couldn't be connected to Jordan and Gabby.

"Baby, listen to me – you have to go. You cannot be here," he said.

"I'm sorry for not listening. I'm sorry you felt that you have to let me have my way and have my space."

"Not now Gabby. Don't apologize, baby. You made it through this, but I have to go. I can't be here and neither can you. You understand that I am breaking apart inside that I have to walk away. Listen, if you need me what have I told you; I would give up my life for you. I will be anywhere you need me to be. Right now, I need to be out of here. I would give up all aspects of my life for you; even my career. Nothing is worth more to me than you. I know you're scared. Ray is here."

Adonis kissed her lips in hopes to calm her down. In an instant, it worked. He felt her relax into his embrace.

"You have to go. I'm going to be fine. Ray will protect me," she finally said.

He smiled at her attempt to reassure and calm him. They were some pair.

"Yes, baby, he will. Let him take you home. I'll be there as fast as I can. Don't worry. You are in the best hands after my own. You trust me?"

"Yes."

"I love you," he said.

"I love you too."

They couldn't continue their expressions of love. Ray pushed him toward his truck which one of Ray's guys had brought over to the lot. Adonis hopped in and to his chagrin, he left his love standing in a lot. He knew he had to go. He couldn't risk the CIA being drawn into his personal drama. He stayed close enough to see Ray whisk Gabby away in a truck he knew belonged to one of his men. A member of his team would stay with Ray's truck to explain what happened. When they sped off down the road, Jordan's detail took over the scene. Adonis headed in the opposite direction. He needed to talk to Cypher.

14

Pulling up to Gabby's condo building, Adonis turned into the underground garage and pulled his truck alongside Gabby's black Range Rover. He was glad that in order to get to her three parking spaces, within the garage, there was another custom-built second garage that was secured by a door only accessible by entering a code that only she had. When they started dating, she had given him the code so that he could check on her truck when he checked on her place. After the door closed down behind him, he sat for a minute to ponder all that had taken place. Never had he been more thankful that his leadership demand he takes time off than this time.

When he asked Ray to make sure she made it home while Jordan wrapped things up at the scene and at the police station, he had also instructed them to make sure her truck was delivered to her garage. It was the only place he could think of to quickly get her truck to without it being seen. Protecting her was all that mattered after the incident some hours ago.

He knew that she was still shaken up after being chased by Brien up the PCH. As he turned the engine in his truck off, he looked down and noticed the slight tremor in his own hands. He'd been cool and calmer than usual while all of the action was taking place. That, he knew, is what made him the agent that he was. This was the first time in his career that he found himself thinking about what he could have lost if Brien had followed through on his plan to end Gabby's life since she didn't choose him. Many of his cases had gotten under his skin, but the way he loved Gabby didn't compare to any of them. She was his life. She was his love. She was his all.

He spent a lot of time kicking himself for wasting years fighting the perfect love. Now that he had her, he had almost lost her. The thought of that still had him unsettled. He placed his hands on the steering wheel to calm his nerves before taking a long deep breath. He needed to be the strong one for her. Tonight, would be the first night in weeks that they'll get to focus on each other and not any looming danger.

With Gabby's career, he knew there would always be fans obsessed with her. No doubt, there would even be some willing to go to the great lengths that Brien had done in order to profess love and devotion to her. From this point on, he would make sure that the security around her would be at a level as if they were protecting the president of the United States. He wanted her to have the life she wanted. Her safety had to come first.

Stepping out of his truck, he walked all around Gabby's truck to check out the damage. Though he originally thought about making sure it got fixed, that was no longer the plan. He'd had time to think on the way to her condo. This truck was done, as far as he was concerned. He didn't want Gabby to have any thoughts that scared her any time she would get in it. In the morning, he would have his own mechanic come and get the truck and fix it up. It was going to be donated to a deserving non-profit organization. Gabby will eventually get a new ride. For now, anywhere she went, either he would take her or her car service would get her where she needed to be. He still had months of being at home. He would, for now, be her private security.

Checking the truck his mind focused on the image of her speeding down the highway in the opposite direction of him with Brien close behind. He shook off that image, still fearful of what could have been.

He exhaled knowing Gabby was fine and Brien was behind bars. If it was up to him, the outcome for Brien would have been totally different. Lucky for Brien, Ray got to him first. His friend knew what could have happened if he didn't. Adonis would have taken his life for sure. His rage was that hot.

Leaving the truck, he headed for the only elevator from her garage, putting in Gabby's code. There were other elevators in the building, but this one only went to her floor. One of their first conversations was going to be about her no longer keeping this place. Though the security was great, he needed her in a place, preferably with him, where nights when they were in town at the same time, he could come home to her.

When the elevator reached the penthouse level where her condo spanned the entire floor, he was surprised to get off and there wasn't a sign of security anywhere. His heart rate went straight to overdrive as he reached for the gun at his waist.

"Where the hell are they?" he mumbled while watching and listening for any movement on the floor. Hearing nothing, before he walked to her condo door to enter the code along with his fingerprint, he reached for his cell and dialed Gabby's number. It went straight to voicemail. His worry raced out of control. He then dialed Ray. The call was answered on the first ring.

"A.D. – what's good?" Ray asked.

"Where the hell are you? I'm at the condo and I don't see anyone. Where is my woman?" he demanded. His eyes continued to scan every open space while his back was to the wall.

"She's home," Ray replied.

"Alone? You're not here? No one is here with her?"

One thing he instructed him to do was to stay with Gabby until he arrived.

"Adonis, man, pull it back a few notches before you have a heart attack. You said to take her home, and I did. I'm here outside the gate. She's inside. She said she was going to relax while she waited for you. Her friend, Victoria is here with her."

"Did you see me pull up and drive into the garage? What gate are you at? There is only one gate to her garage. I saw no one when I pulled up."

There was a pause and he waited.

"Dude, where are you? At the condo?" Ray asked.

"Where the hell else would I be if you were taking her home?"

"Man, there is a serious case of miscommunication happening. When you said take her home, I started to head toward her condo and she asked me where I was going. I said you told me to take her home. She said her home wasn't the condo anymore. She said her home was your house; the place she's been staying ever since she arrived back in L.A. Those were her exact words. We're at your house; or y'all house. Look, she's safe. I'm here waiting on you. I've got guys all over

184

this place; up and down the road. We're at the right place; seems like you aren't though."

Adonis dropped his head, put his gun back on his hip and sighed loudly with relief.

"I didn't think about that."

"Neither did I until she cleared it up for me. I asked if she wanted to go by the condo to get anything."

"What did she say? I'm here and can get whatever she needs."

"She told me that she had all she needed at your house, especially after you got home. She's worried about you. I suggest you make yourself ghost from that place and get here to your woman. You should know I got this situation under lock without question," Ray asserted.

"Yeah, I know. It's just, after tonight, I'm still a little on edge. I called her cell and she didn't answer. I didn't see anyone here. My mind went to the worst possible scenario that perhaps Brien wasn't working alone."

"Bro, I got you. Your agent brain was all in your thoughts. Trust me, she is good. I think her phone may be in the truck. She mentioned she never took it out. It may have fallen on the floor of the truck or something. My guys would have mentioned it if they had seen it in the truck when they dropped it off. If you want, I can get someone over there to check it out."

"No worries. I got this. I'll check it. I'm on my way. Thanks for looking after my heart."

"Anytime you need me, I'm here. You know, now that I've decided to stay here in L.A., I'm thinking of starting my own security firm. That has been my plan for years while I was in the service. Now that I'm out, I've learned a lot since you asked me to take point in looking after your lady. You rallied a nice group of guys who I think would be great on my team. I'll keep you posted."

"Good to hear because with her being on the road, I need a new team for her. The last one sucked. I need people I trust with her life around her, especially when I'm not in town because of work. Anything I can do to help, let me know. See you in a minute."

His phone vibrated before he had a chance to put it away. It was Jordan.

"Bro, I've been calling Gabby – what gives?" Jordan asked.

Adonis could hear the worry in his voice. It sounded a lot like his own voice when he was perplexed about her location.

"I understand, man. She's at my house. Her phone may be in her truck. I'm at her condo checking things out. I'll check her car as soon as I get back to the garage."

"Can you go back in and put her on the phone? I just want to hear her voice before I shut it down for the night. I feel like I need to continually apologize for not knowing how obsessed with her Brien was. This is my fault for bringing him into our lives."

"You couldn't have known. He hid it well. Before his obsession with her, there were no signs or cases in his past that had been reported. Gabby knows that and doesn't blame you. She's actually at my house. I thought she was here too, but she wanted to go to my house instead."

"Ah, ha – that's what I was hoping. It's about damn time. She mentioned something about it earlier today. Both of you have been acting like I didn't know. I told you already, there is no better guy for her than you. My dad is on his way here. His plane should be landing in a few hours. He'll be just as happy as I am that the two of you finally found your way to each other."

"Your Pops is cool with me and Gabby?"

"He's more than okay with it. Not only do I know that she'll be loved beyond her wildest dreams, but there isn't a safer place for her than with you. None of us really thought much about what life would be like for Gabby in this political family. We were so busy with our careers that we just assumed she was good. I saw her spiraling out of control with the wild parties and after concert shenanigans. I attributed it all to her feeling free and away from politics. My mother was thinking of giving up being by my father's side in his political career and sticking close to Gabby with her travel schedule. I was thinking that maybe I need to focus more on her and the family and not follow my father and brother into politics. Life was much simpler as a lawyer."

"None of you have to do that. You don't need to make changes if the reason is for Gabby's sake and safety. I'm thinking of making some changes. I love her and nothing is going to keep me from looking after my woman. She is my number one priority. We'll figure it out. First, I need to talk to Gabby about what's next for us. A lot of time has gone by without having her in my life. I don't plan for that to ever happen again."

Adonis reached the garage and went straight for her truck. Opening the door, he felt around while he listened to Jordan confirm how much his family loved the idea of Gabby in love with him.

"I know you would do anything for Gabby. I appreciate that."

"For sure. I found Gabby's phone while we're talking. It was under the passenger seat of her truck. I'll take it to her. Do you want her to call you when I get to the house?"

"No. I wanted to know that she as okay. As long as she's with you, I know that she is. I'm still dealing with the aftermath of the nightmare on the PCH. I'm heading into a local television station to do a press conference."

"Did anyone catch you tackling Brien with those jabs? Brother, you were letting him have it," Adonis joked. "I know it's no laughing matter, but I felt each one of those punches. I would have done worse. I'm glad I didn't."

"True. No one caught it. According to my security, because of how he was crunched down on the side of the truck closest to the sidewalk right near a wall, no one saw it happening. There wasn't enough time for anyone to record it. Besides, all eyes seemed to have been on the commotion as opposed to me knocking him out. I completely forgot that I'm the governor of the state. All I saw was him trying to hurt my sister. Even if someone had recorded it or even saw it, I wouldn't care. This is my sister and she was in danger. Have her call me in the morning. I was planning to stop by late afternoon."

"That's good timing. I was planning to pop some steaks on the grill and spend the day around the pool. You in? Think your parents will want to come by?"

"You cooking steaks? Definitely. I'll let them know in the morning that we're spending the evening with you and Gabby at the house."

"Tell me again how long you are home for?" Jordan asked.

"Roughly six months or so. That's the minimum. It depends on when I get the call from my director for my next assignment."

"Cool. We need a plan for Gabby when you leave."

"I'm already on that. At least I'll be here taking point for the final leg of her tour right here in Los Angeles. There is time to discuss what's next after that. This tour has taken a lot out of her. She has an opportunity to take some time away from singing to do some writing for other artists. She's been busy doing that the past few weeks. She told me she enjoys that more than being on stage. We can talk to her about it tomorrow. I'm going to head home. We good?"

"We are better than good. Thanks for looking after my sister."

"I love her," Adonis replied quickly, without any reservation.

"Thank you for loving her."

"I am the lucky one."

Ending the call, Adonis hopped in his truck and raced to get to Gabby. He knew her and Victoria would be up for hours catching up on all that's been going on. He would give them that space. All he needed was for her to be close tonight. All she would have to do after her night of catching up would be to come upstairs to their bed. That's where she will find him with open arms waiting to hold, kiss and love her.

15

Gabby heard the security system alert signaling that the front door of the house had been opened. She and Victoria had been up late talking for hours. When both of them yawned together a few times in a row, they knew it was time to call it a night.

After the incident earlier in the evening with Brien, Ray had sent a car to pick Victoria up. Gabby wanted to go home and out of the public eyes. There was no telling if anyone had yet started to spread the news about what happened while tossing her name in the midst.

As soon as Victoria arrived, they stood hugging in the main foyer for over five minutes. They had talked on the phone for her entire ride from the airport to the house. Gabby didn't want to hit her with everything once she got to the house. Besides, the original plan was for Victoria to be picked up by her, not by a driver. She knew her friend would be concerned.

After eating some delicious leftovers from the evening before when Adonis had cooked dinner, they sat and talked about all that had happened. To say that Victoria was stunned was an understatement. She too had encountered Brien and did not suspect that the perpetrator was him.

Finally, the need to sleep hit Victoria after her five-hour flight from New York. She put her up in the guest room almost an hour ago. That room was no longer being used since her place was now in the bed she had been sharing with Adonis. She was thinking of that being a permanent situation for them.

Excitement raced through her as she sprinted from the bedroom and down the stairs. The only person entering the house at this hour had to be Adonis. She wanted to shout with glee, but didn't want to wake up Victoria. It was three o'clock in the morning. She should be asleep, as well, but there was no way she was going to close her eyes until they first landed on her love. Ray told her hours ago that he was on his way. She started to worry when he hadn't shown up, but Ray assured her he was fine.

"Gabby?" she heard him call out for her.

Seeing him, she couldn't hold back the tears that fell from her eyes. She tried being strong. There was no way to contain her relief at seeing his handsome face. Nothing mattered but him. Before he could call for her again, his head turned in her direction. He must have heard her moving down the steps. Adonis could hear a pin drop if she had one in her hand. He was keen to sound that way.

After spotting her on the steps, she raced across the hardwood floor and right into his arms. She wrapped her legs around his waist and held on. When his hands cupped her behind, she kissed his lips, unable to stop herself from going at him like a crazed woman.

With his mouth, she loved how he possessed her. Adonis, in his own fervor, was going at her lips as if they hadn't seen each other in months. He had to be feeling the same type of relief that she was feeling. If things had been different, she may have never had a chance to touch, feel or kiss him like this again.

"What took you so long?" she asked against his lips.

"I went to the condo. I was then on my way here when I got a call that I needed to head back to the CIA office. I had made a brief call about what happened in case there were images of me in the midst of it all. I got an immediate call to do an in-person check-in. That took longer than I thought."

"Oh."

Gabby was worried. He may have gotten in trouble being a part of a non-sanctioned incident.

"I see the worry on your face. Don't do that. It's fine; it's all fine. I'm just leaving there and came straight here. I was worried when I got to the condo and you weren't there. I told Raymond to make sure you got home."

"I am home," she answered quickly.

"I know that now. I wasn't sure what would happen next. I love having you here with me."

"I love being here with you. I love you."

"And I love you. Does this mean you're staying for good? I can wake up to you every morning? I can make love to you every night?" he asked against her lips.

The way Adonis used his mouth to slowly caress hers, she couldn't wait to indulge in this kind of passion with him day and night.

"For that last thing, I'm thinking every night and all day. You've turned me into some kind of nympho already when it comes to having you love me like you do. I'm sorry you went to the condo. I really thought that when you told Ray to make sure I got home, you meant this home."

She looked at him questionably. Her hope was that they were on the same page.

"Baby, you weren't wrong. We hadn't discussed what would be next for us in the light of day. All this mess with that clown is over; I will never say his name again. Of course, I want you here. More than that, I just want you. I could have lost you. I could have risked all of this by not letting my heart and love for you lead me to you like this."

"It's okay. I think we had to get here this way. I was so immature back then. I was eighteen with a crush that I've had since I was fifteen years old. You did the right thing turning me down prom night. It hurt, but I have you now. You're all mine and I'm all yours. There isn't another place for me but right here with you."

"Damn right!" Adonis shouted before Gabby put her hand over his mouth. She turned her head toward the door of the guest bedroom.

"We have a guest," she whispered.

"Victoria?"

"Are you okay with that? I didn't want her to have to stay at a hotel. I thought about letting her chill at my condo while she's here to give her some space. Then I realized I wanted to have her close by."

"Babe, she can stay as long as she likes. The guest room is now vacant. Is all of your stuff upstairs?"

Adonis asked the question while walking toward the steps with her in his arms.

"Yes, but still not put away. I know you like to dress all sharp and stuff, but I had no idea you had so many clothes, shoes and especially sneakers and boots. Just, wow! I mentioned I wanted to rearrange things a bit and you told me to take my time. I was thinking about all that I have; not just what's here at the house. What are we going to do when I bring all of my clothes and shoes here? Do you know I have a bedroom at my condo that's a walk-in closet attached to what was already a large walk-in closet when I bought it?"

"Well, tonight, you won't need any clothes. You won't even need this little nightie you have on. If you need a room to turn into a walk-in closet, there are two extra bedrooms up here; pick one and it's all yours."

Before she could answer, Gabby saw a change in the look on his face right. It was noticeable right after he rushed them up the stairs to the bedroom. He placed her down on the floor right after they entered the room. She looked up at him. After he closed the door behind them, she pulled him close before he could walk around her. There was no doubt that she had learned to read his emotions and his movements. Adonis was avoiding eye contact so that she couldn't see that he was still off-kilter over what happened. So was she. The difference was, with him, she felt safe and didn't have a care in the world. She needed him to feel the same way.

"I'm okay," she whispered against his neck as he pulled her even tighter.

"You almost weren't."

Gabby heard his voice crack. She held onto him, locking her fingers together behind his back. They stood like that for what seemed an eternity.

"Because of you, I am. If you hadn't been on the case, I don't know what would have happened. It wouldn't be this. It wouldn't be me holding you like this. You are my safe space. It used to be that you were my safe space in my head. Now, you're here, I love you and I'm okay."

"Do you know the hell that would have been my life if things had turned out different?"

Gabby moved her head away from his chest and locked eyes with his when he looked down at her.

"It didn't. Touch me, feel me and then love me. You'll know for sure that I'm right here. Let go of what could have happened. I was completely shaken up until I raced into your arms. That was the moment that I knew everything was going to be alright. I want to be that for you every time you come home to me. I want to be that place where you find the most peace. If you want to hold me like this for hours, I'll stand right here, just like this. If you want kisses on top of kisses, I've got that for you. If you need to love me until you're exhausted, I want that kind of love from and for you. I know you worry about me, but I worry about you holding back or hiding your feelings from me. Don't do that. I am here," she explained.

"I know. I'm just making my way through the feelings."

"Do you go through this with your cases? After, are you usually in a tight knot like you are now?"

"No, not like this. Gabby, this is you. That was you I saw with terror on her face as you drove by me, speeding, waving your hand out of the car while trying to keep it on the road. I can't let go of that. I'm trying. All I need is you; now and forever baby."

Adonis cupped her face and kissed her lips. There was so much passion in his eyes and in the touch of his lips that she felt on the brink of tears herself. She didn't think she'd ever be here with him like this. He has always been the only man she's ever loved; he always will be.

"You got that. With me, I'm not going anywhere."

"Marry me," Adonis blurted out.

Gabby stopped breathing. She held her breath afraid that if she let it go, what she had just heard would be a dream. In his eyes, she saw his truth. They were a mirror of hers and what was in her heart.

"Tomorrow?" she asked and smiled.

When he smiled down at her showing all of his pearly white teeth, the mood was less tense and filled with more love.

"Baby, no, not tomorrow," he laughed.

"No? Why not? You asked, my answer is a resounding yes!" she screamed.

"Okay, go ahead and scream and have Victoria think we're in the throes of something nasty and sexy. You're a screamer and that word sounded familiar," he quipped.

"Whatever. If anyone knows that I don't care if the world hears us making love, she does. She doesn't care. She's begging me to have you introduce her to one of your friends."

"She needs to meet Ray," Adonis suggested.

"I said the same thing. Okay, I lied she may not have begged. I think that's how I heard it in my own head. I like him for her too. Can you make that love connection with them happen?"

"Tonight, the only love connection I'm interested in is one with you. Now, back to this marriage thing. I know it sounded kind of haphazard the way I just tossed it out there with no ring or anything. I'm not on one knee, though I can be in the next second. I will be once I have a ring in my hand. That will be remedied tomorrow. I love you so much and I don't want to play house with you. I'm not trying to take any part of your career away by asking you to marry me. I will support you all the way; it's me and you. I want to do things right. I already know that I'll never want anyone other than you. I've waited too long already. Besides, you've been in love with me since you were fifteen years old. It's time I reciprocated in a way that lets you know I'm where you've always been. I'm sorry it took me so long."

"Too long is right. I'm happy it's happening now; at this point in my life. I would marry you right this second. I was serious about marrying you tomorrow. We can do that, you know. I think my brother can even marry us. Can't lawyers do that?" she joked.

"I don't think it works like that. Besides, don't you want a big wedding with hundreds of people like politicians and Hollywood people? I assume you want the long white gown, too many bridesmaids and all the other stuff that comes with that."

"Me? I know I'm a diva, you don't have to say it. When it comes to you, I'm just Gabby. Besides, let's not get ahead of ourselves with all that public stuff. You have a career just like I do. I would never want to do anything that could risk what you do. I may not know the specifics of your job, but I know your anonymity is what keeps you alive. That's the only thing that's important to me. Marrying you and making sure you come home to me after every case you work on. I don't need all of that. I just need you. Okay, I was rushing the gun when I said tomorrow, but that's how much I can't wait to be your wife. Everything else, we will figure it out."

"Gabby, there is a lot that comes with being married to an agent. I'll be gone months at a time, often with no contact. I will handle that by making sure you have a satellite phone to reach me and only me. We need to have a lengthy conversation about what this all means. You may change your mind once you hear what life with me would be like."

"No, I will never change my mind. Life with you is all I want. I've gotten a small taste of life with you and I wouldn't change a thing. I have no doubts. That will never change. You, yourself, mentioned how long I've been in love with you. Do you really think I'm ever going to decide that I don't want to be with you for any reason? Hell no! You're mine. I will marry you anytime and anywhere. I don't care if it's a lot of people or just the two of us. I want to be your wife, unconditionally. How's that?"

Adonis didn't answer her. He simply picked her back up into his arms and carried her over to the bed. Even though they were in the dark, she was glad she'd left the blinds that hung in front of the balcony door open. The bright moon allowed her to still see all of him. The night was peaceful. All she heard was the sound of their kissing and their hands fighting for who could remove the belt of his jeans the fastest. It was clear to her that Adonis was done talking. He needed her. The feeling and intent were mutual.

Adonis' mouth loved all over hers. She was losing patience with how much time it was taking for him to join their bodies.

"Baby, slow down," Adonis said chuckling.

"Mmm, if you would move your hands and let me get to you, I would."

"We have a house guest, baby, remember?" he asked.

"I do and I don't care. I won't scream. That's the only thing I can promise. I still want the kind of vigorous, uninhibited kind of love I'm now used to with you."

"You greeting me with a nightie and no panties will do it every time," he spoke and laughed against her lips. When his light tap on her bare behind caused her to giggle, he felt every part of his body harden even more at the thought that she was his; finally, Gabby was his.

When he moved his hands away from his belt, she smiled when he allowed her to break the kiss in order to focus on getting his pants off. As he kicked his shoes off and slid his pants and boxers down his legs, she made haste of the thin material of her nightie that she donned as she waited for him to get home. Her original plan was to be naked. Then she thought about Victoria being in the house. She also wasn't sure that Adonis would arrive home alone. There was always the idea that her brother would come with her to make sure she was doing fine. She amazed herself of how quickly she tossed aside what happened. An image of being in Adonis' arms kept her sanity in place.

Her eyes landed back on Adonis who surprised her with how quickly he was able to get naked.

"Well, damn! The many nights since I was eighteen of me dreaming of seeing you like this actually coming true has been my life's greatest wow moment each and every time I've seen you like this."

Gabby crooned when he slowly slid his way up her body, making sure to kiss every part of her. Her excitement grew knowing that she was seconds away from feeling him move in and out of her. Now that she was on birth control, something she took care of a few weeks ago, they no longer worried about condoms. To her delight, the feeling of him in the flesh was worth waiting all these years for.

When his mouth covered her breast, she caressed his head with both hands, encouraging him on and wiggling her hips to let him know how ready she was for him.

"Mine always, my sweetest temptation," Adonis whispered in her ear the moment he aligned his body with hers. She felt his hands caressing her legs as he spread them in anticipation of them finding happiness in each other.

"Always one, baby," she replied.

More words escaped her at the feel of that strong, thick part of him as he slid inside of her body. Adonis brought her the love and peace she knew she would find with him. She'd always known it was him. He may call her his sweetest temptation, but from the moment her brother first brought him to their house announcing their friendship, he had been her sweetest temptation.

With his head pressed between her head and her shoulder, she held him close. As he began to move with slow, smooth strokes, she made sure her body followed his lead and met him stroke for stroke. She was happy that it was Adonis who taught her how to love him back the way he enjoyed. There wasn't a time where he didn't let her know that even with her inexperience, she pleased him beyond what he'd ever experienced before. That, she knew, was love. They were enjoying the motions, but it wasn't about that. Their affection was much deeper than that. It had been since he first kissed her.

As they moved together and his words of love caressed her ear, her hands moved across his shoulders to his back. Lovingly, her nails dug lightly into his back. She knew he loved when she did that. When his hips began moving more intensely, she was on for the ride of her life. Over his shoulder, she could see his hips moving. The sight tingled her womanhood as it combined with the feel of him hard and strong loving her.

She wanted to move into a position with her on top, but she knew Adonis needed this. He needed to know that she was here, she was his. After all that earlier in the evening had produced, she was alive and well. He needed to love her his way.

Her body began to respond with an impending orgasm that she wished would hold off. She didn't want to experience her release just yet, but Adonis' loving couldn't be tamed. Her reaction to him couldn't be prolonged. Nothing erased what happened like knowing the safety she felt cocooned in his love.

Her hips moved wildly under him as his strokes increased in speed. Adonis grunted and leaned up the moment he felt her orgasm. She kept her eyes open like her heart. She wanted and needed him to look in her eyes and find solace. Her body screamed and creamed for him as she thrashed about, trying her best to not wake up Victoria.

In an instant, the stars that cascaded across her eyes and in her head wouldn't allow her to hold back her scream. Her body had a mind of its own and it was hollering for her to holler with it. Before her scream could reach his ears, Adonis' mouth covered hers. Inside of his mouth, he enveloped her yelps allowing her to freely enjoy her release. Before the kiss ended, above her, Adonis shattered, moaning with a grizzly growl. His body didn't slow through the intoxicating madness of their loving. They continued to love just like that until their bodies calmed. She held him close as he rested lightly on top of her.

"It's a good thing you're on birth control because I swear, that was a baby-making orgasm!" he bragged.

Gabby laughed almost as loud as her screams of pleasure usually were.

"I can't wait to have your babies. I want a lot of them," she uttered against his cheek when he rolled them over to face each other while laying on their sides. He moved her leg and turned her in a way that no part of him was pressing into her, but yet, he remained inside of her. That was something she picked up on early. He loved staying intimately inside of her until he had to move.

Though they had just experienced equal explosions, she could feel him hardening again. She wished she could have been experiencing this for years, but not with any other man. It had to be Adonis.

"A lot?" he questioned. "What's a lot? You do realize you have a career, right? In fact, in two days, you will begin the first night of the last three nights of your eight-month tour. What will you do with all of that free time?"

"This! A lot more of this," she proclaimed, moving her body to show him exactly what she meant.

"How do you go from being a virgin a month ago to having a sex drive as fierce as mine?"

"Because it's you; you're my dream man. I've held these legs closed for a lot of years waiting for you. Now that you're between them, you have so much time to make up for. As for what I'm going to do after the tour ends in less than a week? I'm going to work on getting my condo on the market."

"Keep it. That way when your friends visit while I'm home, they will have a free place to stay. When I'm not here, you'll have them here with you to keep you company. If Victoria decides to move here like I suspect she is still thinking about doing, the condo would be a great place for her to live until she is ready to buy her own place."

"That's a great idea. Okay, then that means I'll have time to focus on getting married. I don't want a big wedding. We can do that one day when you're no longer an agent. We may be four or five kids in by then, but I'm okay with that. The media would be all over a wedding with me in it. That would also expose you. Just as you vow to keep me safe, I will do my part to keep you safe too."

Adonis reached over and moved her long hair out of her face so that his lips could easily get to hers. She smiled during and after the deep, penetrating kiss. One thing was for sure; her man loved kissing her a lot and she loved it.

"What about your family? You're the only daughter. They will want a big wedding for you. I don't want to start off with your mother giving me a side-eye for not getting the wedding she's probably been planning in her head for a lot of years."

"I know my mother. She may want that, but she also knows how I feel about you. She knows what you do for a living. We all want what's best to secure that you always coming home to me safely. This is my life; my life with you. I could marry you in a shed. What matters is that I'll be your wife and the mother of your babies."

Adonis laughed.

"You keep pushing this babies, plural thing. Babies on the road is going to be tricky; especially with me on assignment."

"You just don't get it. This is what I want. I want to savor every part of what I've always wanted. That means my career and you. Most important of those is you. I've wanted to always love and be loved by you. I love my career, but it really was a substitute until you came to your senses. Now that you have, I want a home and life with you. I want a family with you. I'm never going to completely give up singing. Thankfully, I know I'll be able to go back to it after I have the life I want for myself."

"Are you sure? I want everything for you that you want for

yourself."

"I'm positive. Now, we have a few more hours before daylight. I'm not sleepy. From what I feel happening down below, you're not tired either," she said, amusing them both.

"Very true. I do want a shower. I was planning to do that before this, but when I'm around you, I can't seem to keep my hands off of you. Make me a promise," he said, sliding out of her body and rolling until she was on top of him.

"Anything," she said softly against his lips.

"Whatever you want or need from me, tell me. I don't care if you think we may have to work harder to keep our love together, I want to know. I haven't been involved with anyone, not seriously, since I became an agent. This relationship and love thing and throwing in distance will be a challenge. Get everything you want out of life. I already know that includes me and my babies. Outside of that, can you handle being honest? I'm speaking about if you want to go back in the studio or do a tour, act in movies, television shows, whatever. Talk to me so that we can work a plan together. Be everything you want to be, baby. I do mean everything."

"I promise you I will do that. First, I want to marry you. That's what's first on my agenda. Can you handle that?"

"Yes, I can. I have something else I'd like to handle in the shower. Join me?"

"You got me up here all hot and ready and you want to stop to take a shower? Now?"

"Baby, wait until you see what I have on tap for you in the shower."

Gabby giggled when Adonis moved with her in his arms and walked into the adjoining bath.

"Whew, yes!" she shouted.

16

Three Years Later

"I swear, this house has the most magnificent view. I tell your father that every time we come for a visit and leave. I still can't get him to buy me a house along the ocean. We spend so much of our time in Washington, D.C., that he thinks it's a waste to spend that kind of money on a house we would never really be in."

Gabby nodded her head, agreeing with her mother. Lois Mann would get that house. Gabby got her determination from her mother. They were alike. She'd been a third party to their conversations about a new house plenty of times. Her father was adamant that now wasn't the time. He did tell her that one day, he would buy her the house she wanted on the water. For now, anytime her mother wanted an ocean view, all she had to do was come for a visit.

With Adonis gone on assignment for the past three months, she loved when her parents came for a visit. Her family made a point of staying close to her anytime he was away.

Adonis was on a deep cover case out of the country. She smiled thinking about the in-depth discussions they had prior to him leaving. He thoroughly prepared her for times when he would be away. Her new security team was in place. With one quick phone call, Ray and his team would be at her door ready to leap into action when needed. Adonis made sure every detail was discussed for her to remain vigilant about her safety and that of their family. He'd seen to everything before he left the house in the middle of the night. Thankfully, as he promised, he gave her a phone that all she had to do was hit one button and he would be on the other end. He told her he didn't care what was going on with his assignment, if she needed to talk to him or just hear his voice, he wanted her to use the phone. There were times when she had to resist calling him just to hear his voice. Him being focused on the task at hand was more important.

"Anybody want a fresh glass of lemonade?" Victoria asked, joining them on the pool patio.

"Me!" Gabby yelled. When her mother said the same, Victoria disappeared back into the house. She had moved to Los Angeles over a year ago. Gabby was glad that they were closer now. As her best friend, they didn't have to worry about only talking on the phone or video chat.

"When is her wedding?" her mother asked.

"She and Ray have decided to do a Las Vegas wedding. They don't have a date yet. They want to do it when Adonis has some downtime since he introduced them."

"Is Ray here?"

"No. One of his guys is outside watching the house. Ray is interviewing some new guys for his security business. He's up to over fifty guys. Word has gotten out in Hollywood about how good they are. He's been expanding by leaps and bounds."

"What's Victoria doing these days since you've stepped

back from your career? I know how much she loved being your assistant."

"She works with Ray, running his L.A. based office. She really loves that. She still works part-time for the record label. When Ray needed help from someone he could trust because of his high-profile clientele, she stepped up to help the man she loves."

"I'm happy for them. I'm also proud of you," Lois said.

Gabby reached over and patted her mother's hand where it rested on the arm of the lounge chair. They were relaxing on the large patio at the back of the house.

"I've always known that."

"You're happy?"

"What? No longer touring?"

"Yes."

"Absolutely. I have never been this happy before. I thought I needed the spotlight to make me happy. I thrived on all of that attention. I mean, who wouldn't. Cameras always flashing, people screaming my name and fans dancing to and singing my songs; that's hard to resist. On the flip side, I discovered more to life than that. My priorities have changed. What makes me the happiest is all of the time I get to spend with you and dad. I have the most loving and sexiest husband who gives me my heart's desires. Best of all, I've got two little people who bring me more joy than I ever could have imagined. Now I know what you have meant all these years when you said that my brothers and I have brought a kind of love and joy to your life that you didn't know was possible. I get it now. Being a mommy myself, I'm all about them. I don't miss anything about the spotlight. I have Adonis. I have Shane and Shiloh. I have all of you. I can't say I don't miss singing.

I'm still planning to make more music. I just needed a little time for me. Thankfully, I don't have to make music just to make money. The plan is to do smaller, more personal shows a few times a month. I don't want my time with my babies taken away. They're only eleven months old. I don't want to miss anything."

"Are we doing a party for their birthday? I can't believe my grandbabies are about to turn one. Time is going by too fast."

Gabby looked over at the pool where her dad was barking out orders to the swim instructors who were on their fourth swim lesson with the twins. Her father loved all of his grandchildren, but there was a special place in his heart for her twins. Every time he could get a break from passing laws in D.C., he and her mother were at her place. Times when her brother Chad could get time off at the same time, they all ended up in Malibu at her house. All the kids were getting a chance to spend time getting to know each other.

"I want to, but I can't if Adonis isn't home. I mean, I could, but I don't want to."

"Have you heard from him?"

Before she could answer, the satellite phone on the table vibrated. The only person calling from that phone would be him.

"Speaking of him, give me a moment. That phone ringing could only be him. Can you keep an eye on the kids? Try to keep dad calm. The instructors are not going to drown my babies. If they passed Adonis' interview with them, I have full faith in them as trainers."

"I got it," Lois said.

As she grabbed the phone and stood to enter the house,

her mother walked to the edge of the pool and sat down.

"Hi, baby!" Gabby said delightfully the second she answered.

"I miss you! I love you!" Adonis declared before he said anything else. She loved when he called or she would call him. Before he said anything else, his first words were always that he loved her.

"I love you, too. Are you okay?" she asked.

She didn't tell him, but she worried about him; even more when he called using the satellite phone.

"I'm perfect. I was missing you and my babies. Are they napping?"

"No. Your little gangsters are wide awake. They're in the middle of their weekly swimming lesson."

"So, Elsa and Michael are working out good with them?"

"Yes. They are perfect. The kids love them. You should see the twins float on their backs. They love the water."

"I knew they would. It's important that kids learn how to swim early. They are their father's children. I can't wait to see them."

"I will have them brought in so that you can video chat with them. You know how much they love seeing and talking to you when you're away."

"Really? That's the only time?" he joked.

"Silly! Of course not. You're calling in the middle of the day, so I assume you want to talk to them. You usually reserve your late-night calls just for me after the twins are down. That's our grown-up, sexy time. My parents are here and can watch the kids if you would prefer me naked right now. I've been thinking about you and that. I can slip away. Victoria is here and can keep them entertained while I lock myself in the bedroom."

"Can you lock me in the bedroom with you, my sweet?"

Hearing his sexy tone had her body going through all kinds of sexy motions.

"If you were here, I would do that without hesitating. You know how I do when you come home. I've been storing up a lot of orgasms that are waiting to be set free the moment you get home."

Gabby turned at the sound of the front door opening. When her eyes landed on Adonis, she forgot all about the stupid phone, throwing it to the floor and running at full speed almost knocking him down. She found herself leaping into his arms, kissing every part of skin she could get to on him.

"How many do you have stored up?" he asked against her lips.

She didn't know anymore because her lips were screaming for more and more of his. It had been a few months since he'd been home. They were masters at making their marriage work with his life away from them often.

"Adonis?" Victoria said coming around the corner from the family room which was between the kitchen and the large open foyer at the entry of the home.

"Hey, sis!" he said, and gave her a high-five. He would have hugged her as he usually did, but Gabby had no plans of releasing her husband to greet anyone. As he and Victoria chatted quickly, she continued kissing every part of his face, loving that he was back to her in one piece. She was also checking his face and hands for scars. The last time he'd come home from an assignment, he had a black eye and several scratches across his cheek. She didn't ask what happened. She only wanted to know that he was okay. He had been. That time, she'd raced upstairs and drew him a hot bath.

"Glad to see you home. Did Ray know?" she asked.

"No. I didn't tell anyone. I wasn't sure I would make it, so I kept this trip to myself. I'm actually home for a while. I have a stateside assignment right here in Los Angeles."

"Really?" Gabby shouted with glee. "How long?"

"At least a year."

"Ah!" Gabby shouted and danced in his arms.

"A year? Ray and I can get married. Wait until he hears that," Victoria said.

"You'll be here for the twins' first birthday. We can have a party!" Gabby added.

"That's why I took this assignment. Another agent took my case which is allowing me some stateside time for a while. We can talk about that later. I have more I want to talk to you about," he said.

Gabby looked at him puzzled. She tried to find signs on his face that trouble was on the horizon.

"Um, do we need to talk right now?" she asked.

"No. We can do it tonight after the babies are in bed. Trust me, it's all good."

She smiled with relief.

"I'm going to finish fixing the kids' lunch," Victoria said as she walked away. "It's good to have you home," she added.

"It's good to be home. I've got plans for you tonight. I want to see the kids first. The way I miss you and them is crazy. When I was told I could come back stateside, the only thing I wanted to do was get to you. One day of debrief in Virginia and a quick five-hour flight and here I am."

Gabby jumped down from his arms and pulled him toward the patio door.

"They're in the pool," she said, following him out.

After hugging her mother, who was just as surprised to see him, she watched Adonis head to the pool. After greeting her father, he leaned down and called the twins' names. After a few seconds of realizing who was calling them, both, with toothy grins, clamored for him. As much as they loved being in the water, they loved their daddy more. They were so excited to see him that she raced over to the pool to help pull them out. They were giving her father and the instructors a fit as they smacked the water in an attempt to grab onto something to reach him. If they didn't soon reach him, she feared Adonis would forget that he was fully clothed and jump in to get to his babies quicker. He was as perfect as a father as he was a husband.

"Whoa, whoa. I got you," Adonis said pulling both kids into his arms.

She loved watching them dance in his arms with excitement. Both fought to grab his neck the tightest. She laughed when their daughter, Shiloh tried to climb up his chest. Their son, Shane did his usual of climbing around to get up on Adonis' shoulders. Even though he spent a lot of time away from them, video chatting often kept them close to him. It was important to them both that the kids see him often. When he was home, he was all about them. The last time he was home for a brief stay of three days, he spent the entire time with her and the twins at the house. The babies slept with them because he didn't want them out of his sight even for a moment. Whenever he left, he had to do so when they were asleep. Shane and Shiloh would scream like crazy if he tried to leave the house without them.

"I guess I'm not the only person happy to see daddy, huh?"

Gabby quipped when they giggled while patting Adonis' face with their little hands.

She tried to squeeze in on their group hug, but neither twin would let her in. They only wanted him. Shiloh whined and pushed her away. Shane just kept telling her no when she asked could she hug daddy too. They were not having it. She knew how they felt. She loved having her family around but now, she selfishly wanted quiet time with Adonis and the kids. She was anxious for the talk he wanted to have.

"I've missed you two. Daddy loves you!" he declared as they play smacked his face together. He was loving all of their attention.

Looking around at the scene before her, family, her loves, her life – this is what she enjoyed waking up to.

Adonis took the kids with him and sat with them, wet and all, in his lap on one of the large lounge chairs. As they all talked, giving him all of the latest information on family happenings, ten minutes later, both kids had fallen asleep in his arms. When she tried to take them to put them to bed, Adonis stopped her. He just wanted to hold them; one on each of his shoulders. She pulled the blanket up higher around the three of them and let him have his moment. Being away had to be hard on him. Their eyes connected and she knew. She could read it. Their talk would be intense. Something told her that something was about to change. Whatever it was, as long as they were together, she was ready. For now, she had him home for what would seem like an eternity in the life of an agent. She was going to soak up every moment of it. This is what she'd prayed for. She got it. Nothing was greater.

**

The house was quiet. Adonis had done one last check on Shane and Shiloh after putting them to bed an hour ago. He rubbed his hands together as he entered the master bedroom knowing, Gabby, in all of her sexiness was waiting for him. He first checked to make sure the video camera in the kids' room allowed him to keep his eye on them throughout the night if he chose to. He loved looking at them and knowing they were his. He grew up not having much of a family until he met Jordan. To have his own wife and kids had him whispering a quiet thanks that this is where his life was now.

Looking toward the bed, he smiled at Gabby who laid wide awake watching him. She allowed him the time with the twins that he needed. That was a norm anytime he was away. Being a dad was something he would forever be grateful to her for. She'd given him two babies who were his world.

"You know, I'm still trying to figure out if you were actually in the delivery room when our kids were born. They look exactly like me. Are you sure you're their mother?" he joked.

"I'll take that. They get my brains and your good looks. I would say that's a perfect combination. They down?" she asked.

"Yeah. They were fighting it though."

"They're excited that you're home. I understand how they feel."

"Weapons secured?" she asked.

Adonis knew she was talking about his guns. He had other ideas though. He grinned at her before watching her eyes as they looked to his crotch. That, he knew was her weapon of choice.

"Yes. They're in the safe locked up. The one weapon you want and need is ready for action," he joked.

Adonis slipped off his boxers and moved close to her in bed. Lifting the blanket, he delighted in her already being naked. When they were in bed together, they loved never worrying about clothes. They preferred all skin for as many years as they could get until the kids were older. Somewhere in the future, they would be bursting into their room unannounced.

"I love how you feel," he said, pulling her body as close to his as he could get.

"I can't believe you're home. I like surprises like today. You know you made my day, right? I couldn't have asked for a more perfect moment than you coming through that door today. I wanted everyone to leave. Is that bad? I love my parents and Victoria, but I don't get enough time with you as it is."

"No, that's not bad. I normally would be on the same page with you, but I know I'm home for a long stint, so it was all good. They wanted my famous steaks on the grill. After my shower, I was more than happy to do that. Ray came by. Jordan came over with his lady. It was our chance to see them all. For at least a week, I don't want to leave this house. I would prefer no one being here but us. When I'm away, I have to stay focused. That means putting thoughts of you and the kids in the back of my mind. When I finally get my arms around all of you, I need that time to just bask in knowing when I'm here, I'm here one hundred percent. I feel like I have so much time to make up for. I hope I'm not being selfish when I get that way. I don't want you to feel caged up in here with me because I miss y'all so much."

Gabby sat up straight.

"Listen to me, husband of mine – I don't care how much

time you feel you need with just me and the kids. You will get that each and every time. Everyone we know already get what life is like when you come home. You don't have to say it. They understand. I understand. Your favorite chef will be here all week cooking our favorite meals. We'll go down to the beach with the kids and let them play with you in the sand. Shiloh still hates the feel of sand under her feet, but Shane loves it. They are walking now and getting into everything. We can plan their first birthday party together. I know you love putting them in the truck and taking long car rides. I'm already mapping that out for some time next week. I want to do all the things you want to do. You do miss a lot when you're gone. It's when you get home that we get to relax as a family. That means a lot to me just as it does for you. Don't feel bad or selfish about wanting us to yourself. I speak for our kids when I say we love it too. Always get what you need from us. You take care of us. You love us. I know you're fighting for more time with us. We're here, baby."

Adonis kissed her sweetly.

"Before I get as much of you as I can get before our babies wake up screaming for us, I want you to know that I've made some decisions. I know we said we would make all decisions together, but this one, baby, I knew would be in the best interest of our family."

"What's going on?"

"You already know I'm taking an assignment here for at least a year."

"Okay. I also know you can't tell me about it, which is okay. Having you home for a full year is more than I could ever ask for. We can go on vacation and just enjoy each other. Will there be time for that?" she asked.

"Yes. I'm thinking of the Amalfi Coast in Italy, for sure. I want to go for at least a month. I was searching for locations to stay while I was on my flight home. I know you've been talking about going with the kids. I've got a few months before my assignment starts."

"That's great news. We can work that into the schedule. We can have the party for the kids and then go on vacation; just the four of us. Is that what you wanted to tell me? That's the decision you made?"

"Not just that. After this assignment, I've put in to stay stateside permanently. I may have to travel to other states, but mostly, I will be right here at home. Before you ask if I did this for you and the kids the answer is yes. I knew it would be hard being away from you. I also know that you have home on lock, so I wasn't worried. I want to be around to watch my kids grow up. I've shared with you what my life was like growing up. I have little to no family that I know of. Parents were non-existent. I don't want that for my kids. I want to be a presence in their life. I need them to know that daddy is and will be here. I love what I do, but it's not the only thing to do. There is a lot I can do that doesn't need to involve me being out of the country for months at a time. I've been offered a position that allows me to be much closer to home. There wasn't much time to decide because the position had not been made public but would have been in a few days. I needed to accept it immediately or it could go to someone else."

"You took it on the spot?" she asked.

"I took it before my director got the last word out of his mouth."

Gabby danced around in the bed. She jumped up and danced from one end of their California King to the other.

"You just keep making a way for me to be happier every single day. I can't believe you're going to be home more often. I can't ask for more than that knowing the sacrifice you're making."

"It's for our family. You've made a big sacrifice for me when you stepped back from your career. I know what that meant to you."

Gabby finally plopped down right on top of him and smothered his face with kisses before kissing him senselessly, claiming his lips as hers.

"You are what means most to me; you and our babies. I told you that over two years ago. I meant it then and I still mean it. You keep us safe and we keep you safe. I love this much quieter life."

"I know you miss music."

"I've been in the studio some this past month getting my vibe back. I never want to tour again, that's for sure. I don't have the love for that kind of attention anymore. Remember the awards show right after we got married where I won for best soul artist of the year?"

"I sure do. You had on that sexy, sexy red gown. You wowed everyone on the red carpet that night."

"I hated that I couldn't have you with me because it could have compromised your undercover work. I was and am happy. You were there, but couldn't be out in the open with me. I was okay with that because I know you love me and support me. If I have to choose, I will always choose you. That's not a step down from anything. I don't feel like I'm losing any part of who I am because I choose you and our kids. How much more money could someone spend in a lifetime? I was in love with the lifestyle I was living. I made millions. I'll never spend it all in my lifetime. Money isn't everything. I know there are a lot of paper chasers in Hollywood, but that number doesn't include me. My greatest joy is taking care of my sweetest temptation, you and my sweetest love, my babies. I still want to write, but I'm focusing on writing songs for others and getting that writer and producer credit. I have all kinds of plans for our family now that you're home."

"Birthday party for the twins on the top of that list?"

"Absolutely. Then it's our trip to Italy. I'm going to love planning it all."

"I'm on board for having you, Shane and Shiloh close. Thanks for giving me the family I've never had. I didn't know how much I've needed you and them in order to make me whole. I will say, for one week, I don't want to focus on anything but you and the kids. I want to watch movies with them, sit out on the patio and out on the beach like you said. I can't wait to feed them breakfast in the morning. I want to run around and chase them everywhere around here now that they are walking."

"Me? Do I get to eat?" Gabby joked.

She loved making fun of his undying love for the twins.

"Baby, you get all of me. I want to cook for you every morning. Pancakes all around for everybody. No housekeeper this week, so call her. Having the chef is good, but not for a week. Call and let him know I've got this. He should get what we'll need. Can you make him a list of what to bring to stock the pantry?"

"I'll do it first thing in the morning."

"We'll still pay them both. Me, you and my babies – that's it."

"My family already knows. When my mom hugged me

before they left, she said for me to reach out to her when our privacy wouldn't be invaded."

Adonis pulled Gabby down on him, placing her legs on either side of him.

"Speaking of privacy. No more talking until after I've had my quality time with you," he said, kissing her slowly, savoring the moment.

"Those words are music to my ears. Love me forever?" she asked.

"I'm tempted to say forever, but even that doesn't seem like enough time considering what we went through to get here. Thanks for never giving up on loving me."

"And I never will," Gabby assured him.

~~

Read about other books coming up and available by Cheryl Barton below.

Leaks, Lies, Lust and Love
The Brothers of Chi-Town, Book 7
***Preorder available ***

Carlos Kincaid is an irresistible, rugged loner who has always been that good guy who finishes last when it comes to women. Just when he is getting his life on track, his Achilles' heel shows up by the name of Everly Robinson. Along with her came memories of their inexhaustible, hot, steamy, lust-filled nights between the sheets.

Everly chose the wrong man one time too many in her life. Now, she's on the run from a dangerous man and in desperate need of help. With nothing but the clothes on her back, she returns to the only man she trusts. Carlos was also the only man she's ever loved despite toying with his heart and leaving him for his best friend.

Carlos is frustrated that old feelings could lead him back into the arms of the woman he needed to hate in order to forgive. He couldn't tell if her story was filled with lies or truths. Unfortunately for him, Everly is still the only woman he wants more than his next breath. Is he willing to risk his heart and his life for a woman who once betrayed him and his love for her?

New Release - The Diner

They had been young and in love after meeting at The Diner. Once Camille and Everett Sumpter became one, they thought their life and love would be perfect. Their eventual divorce shattered every dream she ever had about happily ever after, especially once Everett had moved on.

Camille is now in her fifties and ready to love again. She didn't expect the focus of her desire to be her ex-husband. After what was an unplanned, one-night stand filled with once unleashed, now rehashed passion, she tried to go back to her life. Thoughts of Everett's sizzling seduction had stoked a fire in her that had been dim for many years. It was now alive again and ready for more, but only with him.

Fate brought them back to The Diner once again. It was where their love first brewed. Camille only has to let go of the past and be willing to partake in the reawakened fire that has ignited a thirst which seems to have never been quenched by any other man.

Come join me at The Diner for a story about love truly standing the test of time.

The Sweetest Revenge – Now available!

Delaney Monroe had a secret. She thirsted for earth-shaking sex that being married for years never provided. Now divorced, she understood the assignment; to live life on her own terms. She'd never experienced the kind of racy, wild intimacy that she'd only dreamed of with her faceless fantasy man. She was sure he possessed all she wants and needs when it comes to her ultimate satisfaction.

Nashall Patterson was famously known for being a happily single, salaciously sexy, and untamable stallion to every woman who has ever set eyes on him. He never had to worry about his heart being on the line because he never involved it when he indulged in women. That was until he met Delaney during a pre-wedding weekend meet and greet for his cousin's upcoming nuptials.

Delaney, the reserved businesswoman, and Nashall, the bad boy of hedonism had no idea that her secret hunger would lead to amorous encounters that were no longer just cravings of the body but drove them to the desires of their hearts as well.

Could what started out as voracious encounters lead to love of a permanent kind?

It Should Have Been You

Karma:

Dr. Clayton Myers was never a believer in karma, but he did believe in fate. Both would soon collide and expose a secret that would impact the perfect life and relationship with the only woman he ever loved, but not the only woman he took to his bed. That revelation would put his life on a path he accepted while never forgetting what could have been.

Disappointment:

Dr. Donna Spencer had experienced one of the darkest days of her life at the hands of the man who made a promise of forever. She took the hit to her heart and realized nothing good lasts forever.

Fate:

After years of no contact, Clayton and Donna's paths would cross again, forcing them to face the past where their love resided, while wondering what should have been and if they could find their way back to love again.

Three's a Crowd
Book 4, The Sullivans of Montana

Businessman Shelton Sullivan was clear that as a kid, he loved life growing up on the Sullivan Ranch wrangling cattle and riding horses. As a man, he prefers big city life, wrangling expensive suits and most of all, riding sexy women. He was blindsided when a woman penetrated the wall of steel that surrounded, what some said was his black heart, when it came to being in love; he preferred lust.

Deputy Sheriff McKenna Gibson needed a fresh start in a new city. Escaping a life that was crafted for her had become old and dull. Sizzling, spicy encounters with Bozeman's most eligible bachelor was exactly what she needed to help her forget the secrets she was hoping to leave behind in her old life as a military wife.

Without warning, Shelton found himself swept up into McKenna's amorous sensualities that very much matched his own dalliances. Their steamy, seductive encounters led to even more explicit and erotic romps until Shelton's world crashed down like a Montana boulder. McKenna is injured in the line of duty and his world is rocked off of its axis when her military husband blew up the love he thought was blossoming from the one time he decided to let down his guard.

Is Shelton willing to forgive and forget and turn away from the red-hot stirring in his chest at the thought of her?

On the Right Track
Book 3, The Sullivans of Montana

Professional race car driver, Dayton Sullivan, is the youngest of the Sullivan boys out of Bozeman, Montana. He's found himself in a bit of a jam when he falls in love with Kima McDonald, the daughter of a man who could be responsible for the death of Kima's mother.

They ran to the Sullivan Ranch in order to escape the life she's being told she has to live to support her father's schemes. It's discovered that her father has debts that can only be settled if he can get Dayton back on the race track and Kima married to a man she doesn't love.
Can their love sustain them through the ups and downs they'll face against her sinister father?

The Way You Love Me
Book 2, The Sullivans of Montana

Montana ranch owner, Perry Sullivan, befriended a woman who finds herself in dire need of his help. He doesn't hesitate to provide shelter and protection the way any man should for a woman who is in distress. What he had not planned on was in the midst of the turmoil that was her life, he would lose his heart and fall in love while at the same time putting the lives of his own family at risk. Gizelle Duncan had a tumultuous past she didn't want anyone to know about, but when that past, in the form of her abusive ex-husband, shows up in her life again, she has no choice but to accept help from one of those sexy Sullivan boys from the Sullivan Ranch. She thought she had lost all faith in real love until Perry showed her that she could trust him not only with her life, but with her heart.

"The Way You Love Me" will take you on a journey from the ashes of Gizelle's burned-out house and life and into the flames of passion that will not be contained even at the peril of a jealous ex-husband out for revenge.

Home for Thanksgiving
Book 1, The Sullivans of Montana

Firefighter Nicholas Sullivan is going home for the holiday after he was sidelined due to an injury on the job. Guilt over a life lost has kept him away from his family's ranch in Montana and now he's forced to face his past demons and deal with a self-imposed life of regret.

Veterinarian Parker Wingate's first encounter with the handsome firefighter was less than pleasurable. She sympathized with his hurt, understood his pain and before long, felt his love.

Knowing the holiday season is ending soon, can Nick go from living in love for the moment to allowing himself to finally live in love forever?

An Unexpected Destiny
Sister Act series, Book 1

Destiny Lockhart's high school crush, Lincoln Cole, is again front and center in her life. She last saw him fifteen years ago when she threw him out of her bedroom after their one night together following the senior prom. That night had been her most embarrassing moment, leaving her feeling ashamed and undesirable.

There was no way entertainment mogul Lincoln Cole could ever forget the shy, yet beautiful butterfly that was Destiny from his years as a high school football star. The now feisty, sexy and self-confident executive who dripped in vibrant, dazzling appeal reminded him that they were never meant to only have a one-night-stand. They were always destined for forever.

For years, they lived on two different coasts unaware that soon, their past would become an unexpected present filled with unfinished desires that once looked like rejection.

For You, I Will
Sister Act series, Book 2

Kasey Young discovered that a man would do anything to keep her in his grips, even if it's her ex-husband. She lived her life his way for years until she'd had enough and filed for divorce. He wants to insert himself back into her life with an ultimatum; take him back or lose custody of their kids. Kasey found herself between a rock and a hard place needing the help of a man she barely knew, but who stirred up deep carnal desires that had been lying dormant.

Attorney Darren Braxton stepped up to the plate to help Kasey with her child custody case as a favor for a friend. What he hadn't planned on was the hedonistic lust for a woman who could cause him to lose all he's gained because he can't say no to her. He did the one thing he could think of to save them both; he married her.

More Than Friends
Sister Act series, Book 3

A storm is brewing in Boston and her name is Nivea Lockhart. Boldly entering into a no-strings affair with her best friend, she thought she could put her true feelings aside. Her mind was on indulging in steamy nights of uncomplicated, noncommittal pleasure. She didn't count on her heart wanting more than that.

Jaxon Hightower is riveted by his best friend, an intense attraction he had done a good job of hiding since their early college years. He thought having a bevy of beauties instead of having her would lessen his attraction and not ruin the friendship he had come to rely on.

After an unexpected, mind-blowing encounter that surprised and shocked their socks off, Nivea and Jaxon danced around the inevitable; true love. They also didn't count on Alicia, the woman who had no plans of letting go of Jaxon without a fight. What she wasn't ready for was Nivea's response to her saying, *It's On!*

About the Author

Cheryl Barton lives in Maryland and in her spare time she loves to read espionage, crime and romance novels, cook, watch Sci-fi movies, spend time with family and friends and enjoy Maryland steamed crabs. Cheryl is celebrating over 30 years as a government employee and loves writing romance novels when she's not working.

Cheryl is the author of over thirty-one romance novels, four inspirational novels and is proud of six book compilation projects with several other incredible women.

Cheryl was a 2019 Finalist for the Emma Award given by Romance Slam Jam and a 2018 Finalist for the Literary Trailblazer of the Year award by the Indie Author Legacy Award. Cheryl is a member of the Contemporary Romance Writers where she currently serves on the board as the secretary.

Connect with Cheryl Barton

Author Cheryl Barton website
www.cherylbarton.net

Pen2Book Publishing House, LLC
www.crbarton.com

Amazon Author Page
www.amazon.com/author/cherylbarton

Blog – It's About the Love
https://mswriterinmd.wordpress.com/

Instagram: @cherylbartonbooks
Twitter: @cbartonbooks
Facebook: @cherylbartonbooks

www.ingramcontent.com/pod-product-compliance
Lightning Source LLC
Chambersburg PA
CBHW030329030726
47499CB00003B/701